LIFE, DESTINY AND THE INVISIBLE THREAD

SUDHIT YADAV

Made with ♥ on the Notion Press Platform
www.notionpress.com

To Mumma,
my lifeline, my strength — this is as much yours
as it is mine.

To my family,
for standing by me in every field, in every phase.

And to all the people — friends, mentors,
strangers —
who shaped me, challenged me, and helped me
become who I am today.

Thank you.

Contents

Contents

Foreword

"Ever Onward, Quietly."

This book took shape during long nights, countless rewrites, and quiet moments of reflection. It is a piece of my heart in many ways.

Preface

This is a story that moves back and forth in time, much like memory itself.

It isn't driven by fast action or big twists — instead, it's about people, places, and moments. About conversations that stay with you, silences that change you, and the invisible thread that quietly connects everything.

If you've ever missed a friend, lost someone too soon, or held on to a memory for years — this is for you.

I hope you read it slowly. I hope something in it stays with you.

— Sudhit Yadav

Acknowledgements

Though I kept it mostly to myself, I had to share it with a few people. Thank you to those souls who knew about it. Even if I barely talked about the novel, whenever I did, you gave me a push. Each of you acted as a driving force. I mean it — thank you.

I'd also like to thank Notion Press Publishing for supporting budding authors like me. Thank you for giving me a platform to share my story with the world.

Prologue

That one moment brought it all back—the memories, the heartbreaks, the stories I thought were over.
It made me realise: some threads, no matter how invisible, are never truly broken.

This is a story about those threads. About friendship, time, and the quiet way life pulls us back—when we least expect it.

Before You Begin

At the end of this book, there's a note from me —
a personal letter, written with a full heart.

But it holds parts of the story you haven't lived yet.
So please, if you can, wait until the final page before
reading it.
Some things are meant to be felt in the right order.

Thank you for choosing to step into this world.
It means more than I can say.

— Sudhit

1

Chapter One

Present Day – April 2031

As I stared at the blinking cursor on my desktop screen, brainstorming different ideas for my next piece of work, I realized I was literally out of ideas. The next thing I heard was the familiar sound of my phone ringing. After letting it buzz on my table for a few seconds, I finally picked it up. It was an unknown number.

"Hello? Who's this?" I inquired.

"Good afternoon, sir! Am I speaking to Mr. Ramit Bansal?" the voice on the other end asked.

"Yes, this is Ramit Bansal speaking," I confirmed, with anticipation starting to build up.

"That's great. I'm Amit Tandon speaking from 'Kick-Start Your Biz,' and you visited our Vasant Vihar branch on 15th March, 2031, right?" Amit asked.

I had been waiting for this phone call for the past month. I had started to think that they'd forgotten, but here it was — they finally called.

"Yes, I remember. I applied for consultancy services provided by your business regarding opening up a restaurant business," I replied, with excitement running through my veins.

"Exactly! Coming to that, I am the person who is assigned to help you get your dream project on-board. I have been working in this industry for a long time, and I know this game inside and out. I'll be assisting you in this whole process," Amit announced.

"I'm glad to hear it. So, when do we start?" I asked, getting up from my chair and pacing the room.

"First of all, we need to find a location for your diner so that we can apply for the licenses required to run it. Do you have any preferences?"

"I am looking for a place, preferably in Central Delhi."

Central Delhi... It has always been very close to my heart. It reminds me of my college days - those were the days. I miss those times so much. I wish I could turn the clock back and go back to that era.

"I know a couple of places down the road. Can we meet some day to check out the locations?" he proposed.

"Just a second, please."

I bent down slightly, resting my hands on my desktop table, holding the phone between my ear and shoulder as I opened up the calendar on my PC. I checked my schedule for the upcoming weekend. "Yeah, let's do it. By the way, are you free this Saturday? Yes... Mm... Okay, done. I'll be there."

I typed down the details in the tasks application while confirming it on the phone call. "12:30 PM, Rajiv Chowk Metro Station, 23rd April."

After the phone call concluded, I leaned back in my chair. I couldn't really think of any great ideas at the moment, especially after this phone call, as a sense of purpose settled over me. I should get some rest and work on this later. I have an important weekend coming up.

I laid down on my bed after shutting down the desktop. After a few minutes, I heard some footsteps approaching my room. The door opened with a slight creaking noise, and Mumma entered my room with a tray bearing a cup of tea and some snacks. She placed it down on the bed and looked at my face as I was completely lost in thought.

"Still no ideas?"

I nodded, replying in a contemplative tone, "Yeah… This and that… The guy from the business consultancy company called. He wants to meet me to discuss the diner location in Central Delhi, to finalize a place for our restaurant."

"When?" she asked, visibly excited.

"This Saturday."

"Finally, it's happening!" She hugged me and kissed my forehead. "I'm so happy for you, *beta*." Her face lit up with pride.

Looking at her joyful face gave me so much warmth. It made my day.

"I'm glad too, Mumma." I picked up the mug. "Thanks for the tea."

"No worries! Drink it before it gets cold."

"I will. I am going to sleep for a while after drinking this. I don't feel so productive today. Need some rest."

"It's okay to feel low sometimes. Get some rest and we'll discuss about your next writing project, once you wake up."

She exited my room, switching off the lights on her way out. I took a couple of sips of tea before going to sleep. It was around 4 PM. If I woke up by 6, I'd still have time to get some tasks done. I set an alarm on my Assistant device, *Ventra,* for 6 PM and enabled the silent mode on my smartphone to avoid any disturbances when I was sleeping.

After a much-needed nap, I woke up at 6 PM and checked my smartphone to see if there were any missed calls or texts. My eyes skimmed through the notifications at a speedy pace and stopped when I read a text from Samarth that said,

Any updates on the restaurant?

Was he spying on me? How in the world did he bring this topic up after I finally received that phone call from Amit? I opened it up and quickly dropped a text:

"Yes! I was about to tell you about this. They called today! We're going out to explore the area this Saturday. You can join us if you're not busy this weekend."

"Ventra, turn on the lights, please," I commanded.

I walked down the stairs to get some water. I reached the kitchen where Mumma was already prepping for tonight's dinner - fried rice tonight. She seemed to be in a good mood lately.

"Did you sleep well?" she asked while chopping the veggies on the slab.

"I did. I feel better now," I replied while gulping down a glass of water. "I don't know why, but I've been lethargic and sleepy for the last few days. I really need to start prioritizing my health."

"The real problem lies within your daily routine. Your sleep schedule is all over the place these days. You work on the computer for long periods, sleep in the morning, wake up in the daytime, work all night, and all that. This is the reason why you are not able to function properly. As I've always said, you should maintain a good sleep schedule. It really helps."

"I agree, but... It's really difficult to get back on track after it gets messed up," I replied.

"I know, *bachha*. But you have to start somewhere, right?"

I nodded. "Do you need any help?"

"I can really use a helping hand out here. Can you please get the dining table ready?"

"Sure."

I stepped out of the kitchen and played some music on the soundbar. It helps me to get going and work productively, while it also adds to the ambiance. After a couple of hours, we sat down at the dining table and discussed my next book.

"What genre are you planning to write now?" she asked eagerly, serving the fried rice.

"I'm not really sure about this. I want to explore the short story genre. I guess I can craft some really intriguing short stories and I just want to take a break from writing long novels for a while. I feel the need to switch to a shorter format before I start working on a bigger novel."

We started eating and discussed further on the possible genres I should try out. I love these conversations where we talk about something that is loved by both of us. I don't think that there has been a single day in our lives in the last few years when we haven't talked about different topics during our dinner time.

Our bond has grown ever since we left her husband - my father, Dinkar Bansal. I still get those dreadful nightmares quite a few times.

After dinner, we watched the TV for a couple of hours before I went back to my room to work for an hour or two and sleep afterward. I checked my smartphone to see a text message from Samarth:

Samarth: WOW! That's awesome! I have an important lecture on Saturday. You know, the exam season is nearby. I am so sorry that I won't be able to join you this weekend, but I promise you that I'll catch up soon. Keep me updated. I'll see you soon.

I voice-texted him back:

Ramit: That's completely okay, Sam. I understand. Hoping to meet you soon! Take care.

I worked on jotting down all the possible ideas for my next books for a couple of hours... and went to sleep.

2
Chapter Two

A Few Days Later – April 2031

"Ramit... Ramit... Wake up! It's already 11:30 A.M. You are supposed to reach Rajiv Chowk in an hour." These words reached my ears, but I was still sleepy.

"Ramit! Wake up!!" Mumma shouted in a louder voice, which made me get up from my slumber in a split second. I looked at the clock and instantly knew I was screwed. I had to get ready in under twenty minutes and reach Vasant Vihar metro station by 11:55 to make it on time. I quickly got out of my blanket and jumped from my bed to get things going.

"I'm going to make you some breakfast while you shower. Would you like some coffee with toast?" Mumma said, fixing my blanket.

"Sounds good. Just make it quick. I can't afford to be late anymore."

I rushed through a quick shower and got ready in almost eighteen minutes. Not bad, though it could have been better than this.

"Here's your breakfast. Don't choke yourself, eat slowly but quickly. I hope you're getting my point."

I quickly gulped down the coffee and finished the toast in approximately six minutes. I kissed Mumma on the forehead and ran toward Vasant Vihar Metro station.

"Good luck, *beta*! Stay safe and don't hurt yourself in a rush! Call me when you get there."

"Thanks, Mumma! I will. Gotta run now!" I shouted, slamming the door and bolting down the stairs. "Sorry!"

I looked at my watch and it was already 12:02 P.M. I sprinted my way to reach the station as soon as possible. That was one long sprint, which lasted for about 4 minutes. Just as I was tapping my DMRC card, my phone rang. It was Amit. I picked up the call.

"Hey, I might be a bit late," I told him, panting. "Running 15-20 minutes behind."

"Actually, same here," he said. "Sorry—I had some tasks I had to finish. I'll be at Rajiv Chowk by 12:55. I'll call you when I reach."

"It's completely okay, Amit. See you soon."

All that rush just to find out he was running late too. I could've savored that toast.

I reached the platform and boarded the metro. It was crowded, even for a weekend. I stood by a corner seat of the coach and opened my phone to scroll through the headlines. I kept glancing up as we approached Dilli Haat-INA. As the train pulled in, I squeezed through the crowd to get out, battling the usual chaos of people boarding before others could exit.

After a long walk and waiting for 3 minutes on the platform, I finally boarded the train going towards Rajiv Chowk at around 12:27. As always, it was a very crowded metro, but I managed to board the train and stand near the doors of the metro. Station after station, a few people boarded, a few people alighted the train, and I finally reached the Rajiv Chowk station.

I've always loved this station so much. There is something majestic about it - the circular center of the station from which you can see through the sky, the constant movement of people in every direction.

How can you not romanticize traveling through the Delhi Metro network?

I called Amit.

"Hello... I'm almost there. ETA five minutes. I'll meet you at Gate 3."

"Okay, I'll wait there," he said, and hung up.

Despite years of changing lines here, I still found the gate maze confusing. After three minutes of wandering, I spotted Gate 3.

"I'm walking toward Gate 3. What are you wearing? How do I spot you?"

I quickly glanced at my outfit. "White polo tee, blue jeans, greyish shoes."

"Green t-shirt, black jeans. I think I see you—turn around. I'm waving."

I turned. A Caucasian man was waving at me.

"Yep, I see you. Come over."

We shook hands.

"Hello, Ramit. Sorry I'm late. Got stuck with other clients. Ready to explore this beautiful area?"

"It's okay, Amit. You can catch your breath for a while before we go out there. I've been waiting for this day since forever. This restaurant means a lot to me."

For the next 2-3 hours, he took me around to the different corners of Connaught Place and showed the available properties. It was going to be a difficult to task to finalize a location. It was overwhelming - so many options. After the tour, we grabbed food at McDonald's.

"I hope you liked the locations. I'll send a list of all the available places to your contact number and email. You can take your time and make a decision that suits you the best. After you decide, we'll move further in this process and start the licensing procedures. It takes some time and a lot of formalities and paperwork. But I'll be there to guide you. Together, we will lay the cornerstone of your diner. It's a process, but I'll guide you. Leave feedback on our site, and I'll see you next week. Have a great day!"

"I'm already having a great day, thanks!" I said. "Thanks for devoting your time today. I'll call you after I discuss it with my family and friends. Safe travels!" I bid him farewell and we both went our separate ways.

I called Mumma from the platform.

"I'm on my way home. Need anything from the market?"

"No, just come back safely," she said.

I got home around 7:30 P.M.

"How was your day, Ramit?"

"It was a really long and tiring day, but we went to so many plots and places in CP to find just the perfect spot. I'll show you the available options as soon as he sends me a complete list. After that, we'll proceed to the paperwork stuff."

"Good to know. Now take some rest. You left home in a hurry. You must be frazzled. I'll make your favorite dinner."

"Woo-hoo! I'm ecstatic today. I love you, Mumma. I'm going to change and we'll talk about it later," I replied in a gleefully.

One small step closer to a big dream.

3
Chapter Three

The Next Week

"This one seems way better than the last one... What do you think?" I asked Mumma, while scrolling through the list and switching between the different tabs opened on my PC.

"Yeah, I think it's great. The only con is that it's a bit more expensive than others."

"I agree. Probably because it is located between two important metro stations. I love it, though. What do you reckon?"

"If you think that this is the right decision, go ahead with it. I like it too. What's Samarth's opinion?" she asked.

"He is thinking either this one or the one on Tolstoy Road. But I don't want to go too far away from CP. I want it to catch eyes. I want it to become one of the most visited diners in Delhi," I told her.

"Let's seal this option. But think about it once or twice more before calling Amit. I don't want you to regret it afterwards," she advised. Well, she's not wrong after all. I should give it a day or two, research about it, a bit more and then lock the option.

"Alright. I'll see about it. You don't need to worry, *Maa*. We'll manage everything. We've been planning this for years. I won't blow it. We're in this together," I assured her.

"I know, *beta*. But you know, it's a huge financial decision. Probably one of the biggest financial decisions of your life, if not the biggest," she said in a low tone.

"I get your point. I understand your concern. But I want you to know that you don't need to stress yourself out. We've been pooling funds for it, and Samarth is going to be my partner in running this. You tell me-do you like this place?"

"I do," she answered.

"Great! You don't need to bother yourself for no reason, okay?"

"Okay," she said and smiled.

"That's like my mother!" I got up from my chair, held her hands to give her a sense of assurance, and hugged her.

"All the very best for this endeavor, Ramit. I'm proud of you, no matter what happens," she said, hugging me tightly.

She left my room as I called Samarth to discuss it for a while. I dialed his number, and he picked it up almost instantly. "Hello, Ramit!"

"Woah! So Quick! I'll assume you were waiting for a phone call," I giggled. "Okay, so I called you to discuss the diner location. We like the one on the left side of Barakhamba Road. What's your take on it?"

"I think it's perfect. But somewhat costlier. I guess we should look for a cheaper option. But if you and Aunt Anubhuti like it, then we can go ahead," he stated.

"I agree on the expenses part. But I feel like it's the most appropriate choice," I said in a convincing manner. I really want this place. I love it.

"Okay, then. If it feels right, let's do it. And you know, I'm standing right by your side," he said gleefully.

"YES! I'll text you or call you when I make a final decision. I'm telling you, when you see it, you'll love it!" I exclaimed.

"I know. I should visit it once, as soon as possible. You free on 1st May?" he asked.

"I've got some work during the daytime, but I can certainly take some time out in the evening. Wanna visit it? I can do it."

"Cool! Let's meet on 1st May, 6 P.M.?"

"Done. I'll call you later. Gotta do some tasks at the moment. See ya soon! Bye!"

"No worries! See you soon. Bye!"

The call ended, and I sat back on my couch, contemplating about it, lost in thought. There's something that feels really special and magical about that location. In the lower right radial area of Connaught Place, the vibes and everything about it are so majestic.

I must get that place.

We'll lay the cornerstone there.

4
Chapter Four

May 2031

"Isn't it beautiful?" I asked Samarth, my eyes fixed on the plot.

"You were right about it. You were absolutely right about everything. This is picture-perfect," he agreed, a smirk on his face.

"This is exactly how I envisioned it. This is impeccable for a restaurant, and you have got to see it from the inside. Come on!" I cried out in excitement.

We both entered the building. It was full of dust for now, but I could already see the huge opportunities lying ahead - the chance to transform it into a fine dining restaurant with a romantic, feel-good ambiance.

"It's huge, too. We can add so many small yet impactful elements to it. Like a stage or something, where singers could try out gigs and elevate the whole vibe," he said thoughtfully.

"I know, right? Here we'll have the kitchen," I pointed at a particular area. "And we can arrange the tables in a stylized pattern in this section," I said, running around the plot in restless excitement.

"The endless possibilities we'll unlock with an area like this. Just imagine, Ramit. Just imagine," Samarth said in awe.

"This is exactly what I was trying to tell you. It's difficult to describe in words or text. I hope you love it."

"I absolutely love it! What do you think, Aunt?"

"It's wonderful. You have my consent," Mumma replied with a smile on her face.

After half an hour of exploring the place, we headed out to have some food at the nearby Haldiram's. We spent some quality time there and had a wonderful chat. On our way back, we waved goodbye to Samarth as he took a cab towards East Delhi. Mumma and I decided to take the metro for some reason, even though we could've had picked a cab too.

We reached the platform and were waiting for the metro.

Suddenly, I felt a hand resting on my left shoulder—and the next moment, I heard a familiar husky voice.

"It's been a while."

I turned around—and froze.

"Ayush?! Ayush Malhotra?" I examined his face, standing there in utter shock. His looks had changed a lot, but I recognized him almost instantly.

The person who used to be one of my best friends during my early adulthood.

The person I used to share all my deepest secrets with.

The person who knew me better than I knew myself.

"You guys know each other? I'm sorry, I didn't recognize you," Mumma said to both of us, noticing my stunned expression.

Honestly, I never thought I would ever see his face again.

"Ramit was my close friend during our college days. He graduated from Hindu; I graduated from Hansraj," he explained to Mumma before I could.

"Oh, I didn't know. Ramit never told me about you. Nice to meet you, Ayush," Mumma said warmly.

Well, she was right. I never told her about him.

Until this moment, when he decided to return to my life unexpectedly.

I didn't know whether I should be angry or simply greet him.

The metro arrived at the platform, and we moved towards it, still talking to Ayush.

"You're going towards Dilli Haat?" Mumma asked Ayush.

"Yes, I am going to change at Central Secretariat. I live in Sarita Vihar," He replied as we boarded the train amidst the crowd bustling in and out.

"How are you, Ayush? You've changed a lot, to be honest. Though I recognized you instantly," I said.

It was a moderately crowded metro, but Mumma found a vacant seat and sat down. We both stood nearby and continued our conversation.

"I'm doing fine, Ramit. We're getting older day by day. Can't resist the changes. How are you?" he asked.

"Never been better. Gotta embrace the changes. What are you doing these days?" I asked.

"I'm an investment banker. After working in an accounting firm, I finally decided to let go of that job and entered this field," he said proudly.

"What about you?"

"Well, I—"

"Ramit is a writer. He's published several novels across different genres, and two or three have become best-sellers. You should read his work—he's so good at it! He's also working on opening up a restaurant," Mumma interrupted before I could even respond.

"Wow! That's interesting. A BMS graduate turned writer. What exactly happened?" he asked.

"I worked in a corporate job before following my passion for writing. I hated my job; I wasn't happy there. It had decent pay, but I wanted to do something I loved. I worked there for almost two years and left it after publishing my third novel, which turned out to be a best-seller."

"Straight out of a movie," he smiled. "I've got to get off at the next station. We should catch up sometime. Do you have my number?"

Yeah, sure. I still have it. In the blocked section.

"I tried to reach you a few months back. But the number was unavailable," he claimed.

No shit, Sherlock. You were blocked.

Blocked since 2024.

"I'll text you on your number. Are you still using the same one?" I asked.

"It's still the same. I'll call you soon. We need to catch up on a lot of unread chapters, right?" he said.

"You're right. Hoping to meet you soon," I replied.

Or maybe not.

"Bye, Aunty! You both should visit my house someday," he said warmly.

"We will surely come over. But you've got to visit our home first. Deal?" Mumma bantered.

"Deal," He chuckled, stepping out as the doors closed.

"He seems like a good boy. How come you never introduced him to me?" Mumma asked.

"He was... until we stopped talking," I said, watching Ayush give me a final glance and a smirk as he disappeared into the crowd.

"Stopped talking? Why?"

"Long story, Mumma. I'll tell you. Maybe some other day. Some other day."

5

Chapter Five

May 2031

Life has been surprising these past few days. Ayush, who used to be one of my best friends in college, has now returned to my life. I never thought I would see him again.

Now that he's back, there's an irresistible urge to revisit the journals I used to write during my college years. I quickly opened my almirah and unlocked the rarely-used locker – Only when I want to go down the memory lane or take a trip of nostalgia. I hadn't opened it in months. After a bit of struggle, I finally managed to pull out the heavy box which contains all the albums, journals and important stuff related to my life. I haven't opened this box since last year, I think.

I placed the heavy box on the ground and quickly dusted it with my cleaning cloth. I opened it up to find some photographs, alongside a bundle of spiral notebooks - my journals. I used to decorate each one of them, so beautifully. I swiftly went through the opening pages of each register to find the one which I used in March 2023. When I first entered Hindu College. One of the most prestigious colleges of Delhi University, where aspirations soar and dreams take flight. I went through a couple of entries to reminisce about the times the memories came rushing back, almost as if I could remember every single detail of what happened during that time.

ϼϼϼ

March 2023

I still remember when I used to think about passing out of school and going to college. Is college life really that exciting? Is it really like the way it's portrayed in Karan Johar movies? Sometimes, I think that nothing could ever top school life. Everything was so simple and easy back then. Things were not so complicated. We used to spend good times with each other—the urge to run towards the ground when the bell rang, going back home while talking about everything, every single day. It was perfect.

I'm not against universities. In fact, I don't even know anything about college life yet. But I know that I'll miss school days a lot.

It's been just two months since our board exams, and I already miss it so much! I hope I'll stay in touch with my school friends. After working so hard for so many days, I finally got admission to a prestigious college of Delhi University. Probably one of the best colleges of India—Hindu College. I had researched about the different colleges of the DU circuit, and Hindu is way up there in the list, at the top.

Today was my first day of college. I was so nervous yet excited at the same time. I reached the Vishwavidyalaya Metro station. They could've come up with a better name; it sounds so old-fashioned. As I stepped out of the Metro station, a swarm of auto rickshaw drivers surrounded us, each naming a different college of the North Campus. One even asked a guy, "Miranda House? Miranda?" That cracked me up. Why would you ask a guy to go to an all-girls college?

I asked a driver to drop me off at Hindu College, and he agreed. I sat in the auto and waited a couple of minutes while they gathered more passengers. I called Mumma in the meantime to tell her I had reached North Campus and was about to head to Hindu in an auto rickshaw.

"Hello there! Fresher?" A fellow passenger beside me greeted me with a handshake.

"Hi! Yeah, Hindu College, BMS 1ˢᵗ Year. What about you?"
I asked, shaking his hand firmly.

"That's great! I'm from Hansraj College, B.Com Honours. Nice to meet you. I'm Ayush. Ayush Malhotra. Your good name?"

"Ramit Bansal. R-A-M-I-T," I spelled it out quickly as people often get confused with my name. The auto rickshaw started speeding through the roads of North Campus as all the other passengers in the auto were looking around in awe at the beautiful buildings we had only seen online or in videos.

"Look, there's Ramjas!" A girl in the auto pointed at the building of Ramjas College. I was so mesmerized by the architecture and the vibes. Everything felt so good! These red-colored buildings were a treat for the eyes.

"Are you on Instagram or LinkedIn?" Ayush asked, scrolling through his phone.

"Yeah… I'm not on LinkedIn yet, but I'm active on other social media platforms, including Instagram."

"What's your username?" he asked.

"@RamitBansal_31," I replied. We reached Hansraj College, and two guys got off the auto, including Ayush.

"You're the first person I have talked to here. I've sent you a follow request. I hope that we'll meet again. Bye, Ramit!" he said.

"I'd be glad to meet you again too. After all, Hansraj and Hindu are not that far apart, I guess. I'll text you later. Goodbye!" I replied, trying to keep things friendly. I don't want to make bad friends, to be very honest. I've heard that you come across a lot of people in college, but not all of them can be trusted.

Some of them might seem like they are so kind-hearted and friendly, but later on, they turn out to be rattlesnakes. I don't want rattlesnakes, not even one. I'll have to be cautious while making friends. I really hate people who are nice when you're in front of them but stab you in the back afterward.

Being an introverted person, it becomes challenging to make new bonds in a new place. I hope everything goes well. The auto rickshaw stopped at the gate of Hindu College. I stepped down from the vehicle to take a proper first glance at the college I'll be attending for the next three years. I reached into my hip pocket for my wallet and paid the driver.

The entry gate was okay, but the college itself was absolutely beautiful. I entered through the gate, and the guards smiled at every new student who came through, asking them to take out our allotment slips. I handed mine to one of those guards, and he greeted me with a smile and returned the slip to me as I started to proceed further.

As an introverted person, I felt it was a bit difficult to settle in social situations like these when I saw some senior girls holding *pooja thalis* in their hands. They welcomed the freshers by marking a tika on our foreheads, saying, "Welcome to Hindu College. All the best for your journey here." I felt elated. I loved how they were so welcoming despite standing in the warm sun, in this hot weather.

I walked further, and the first thought that struck my mind was just how massive this campus is. It's massive. It could easily fit 4-5 schools inside.

"Even my school was bigger than this old-age college," I overheard a girl say to her friend. The audacity to speak something so disrespectful toward a prestigious college like this bothered me. But I already loved this college.

I spent the next 15-20 minutes roaming here and there, admiring the spectacle.

As I made my way to the Sanganeria Auditorium (which is absolutely huge, by the way), I found many new faces waiting for the orientation program to start. For some reason, I started to feel anxious. I searched for a seat and took one that was at the end of a row. I probably did this to avoid people. I was sweating as though I had just played a football match. Soon, several guys came up to me and introduced themselves, along with their courses they got enrolled in. I tried to initiate some conversations too, and I think I did a decent job.

The orientation was amazing as we were welcomed by the principal and the faculty members. They told us about the different facilities available in this college, and I was still amazed by the fact that this college has almost each and every single amenity available, including a freakin' research center. How awesome is that?

In the next few days, I traveled back and forth between home and college, attending almost every lecture. I tried making friends, and I met a cool guy named Samarth Katreja, from B.Com Honours. He's an aspiring chartered accountant and is preparing for his CA Foundation Exam in June.

When I first met him, I was looking for a particular room, where I was supposed to reach at the time and give the first interview of my life. I had applied to join Meraki, the social entrepreneurship society of our college, and I surprisingly got through the preliminary rounds, which consisted of filling out an application form and participating in a group discussion round.

"Hey! Do you know where room number 74 is? I've been searching for it forever but can't find it," Samarth asked me.

"You know what? I'm looking for it too!" I laughed. "Have you also applied for Meraki?" I questioned him.

"Yes! I have my interview today. You too?"

"Bingo! You're correct, and I'm already late. They haven't even told us the exact location of this room, yet expect us to be on time!" I ranted.

We somehow managed to reach there with the help of a few seniors and janitors. We exchanged phone numbers after our interviews ended. I barely know 15 people from my own class, but I certainly know Samarth more than anybody else in the entire college so far.

I tried every item in the cafeteria menu of our college, went on random walks to explore the beautiful campus. Day in, day out- same routine. It's starting to feel a bit repetitive now. I want to experience something new, even though I believe that every day holds a fresh experience. It feels like I'm not sucking the nectar out of my college life. Sometimes, when I look at others on campus, getting involved in conversations with others, making connections so easily without any difficulties, it makes me sorrowful. I hope things will get better with time.

College life is complicated. School life was simple and easy.

I felt like I was finally settling in. I had made some friends - some good friends. I knew most of the classmates by now. I had a decent relationship with the Class Representative too, which would definitely help me to survive college life.

The social entrepreneurship society recruitment results were going to come out today. I was very excited and nervous at the same time. I had only two classes today - and I was running late. I had to reach college in the next 13 minutes, or else the Business Analytics Professor, who was strict, wouldn't let me in.

Somehow, I made it in time and attended both lectures. They were, honestly, very boring.

"Hey! Wanna go to the cafeteria?" Lokesh, a fellow classmate, asked me from behind as I was stuffing my books into my bag.

"Yeah, Sure!" I replied enthusiastically. At least someone was concerned about me.

As we started walking towards the cafeteria through the vast campus, Lokesh asked, "So, have you started studying yet?"

"Study? Study for what? The semester started only 16 days ago," I said, chuckling.

"I mean for the university examinations. Even though the seniors say that even if we start preparing ourselves a night before the exam, we can still achieve good grades. I don't really believe that. How is that even possible?" he said, looking genuinely worried.

Well, he had a point. When I looked at the seniors, most of them were like that – casual about the exams, boasting how easy it was to pass even with last-minute preparations. Why would I even want to leave things until the last moment and risk it? It was better to start slow and steady, instead of panicking later.

"I haven't really started yet either. But honestly, it shouldn't be that hard. I think it won't be too difficult to prepare for these exams, as we studied most of the syllabus during our last two years in school," I said, glancing at him.

Seeing him still worried and anxious, I added, "Come on, don't be worried. We're in college now - a time that will never come back in our lives. Never! This is the first year, and as they say, first year is the most fun-filled phase of one's college life. It's supposed to be one of the best phases of our lives. Let's enjoy this phase, with fewer worries and more joy," I said enthusiastically.

A smile slowly appeared on Lokesh's face. "I guess you're right. This is going to be the time of our lives!" he exclaimed loudly with zeal, causing several heads to turn towards us. He giggled and started running toward the cafeteria. I laughed and chased after him.

We reached the café and found some familiar faces. It was really surprising how quickly friend groups had already formed in the college. Some were from our course too.

I bet most of these groups wouldn't even survive a year.

And again, there were *those* guys – desperately trying to show off their non-existent rizz in front of girls. Cringe.

We ordered some food and, luckily, found a vacant table. It was a crowded day, and the café was packed.

"Where do you live?" Lokesh asked as I looked around the canteen.

"Vasant Vihar. What about you?"

"Well, I'm staying in a PG nearby. I left Madhya Pradesh to study here. I miss home," he said quietly.

"Oh, so you're not a Delhiite. Have you explored Delhi yet?" I asked.

"I did. Some parts of it, when my parents came to drop me off. It was such an emotional day. You know, waving them goodbye, not sure when you're going to see them again. I cried. They cried. We all cried. It was hard." His voice dropped, and I could see the sadness in his eyes.

"You're lucky to live with your parents," he added.

I paused.

"I can truly understand your pain. It's hard to live miles away from your family, on your own, in a city where you don't know anyone — a city full of strangers. But now you know me! If there's anything you need help with, or talk to someone, I'll be there. Okay?" I assured him.

Even though, in my mind, I reminded myself to be cautious about making promises too soon. He seemed like a good guy, at least till now. I hoped we'd be good friends in the future.

"Thank you," Lokesh said, flashing a grateful smile.

As we started eating our meals, a guy rushed past our table, telling something to his friend in a loud voice, "The society results are out! I made it!"

The results! I had completely forgotten about them.

In a panic, I quickly pulled out my phone. Lokesh leaned over my shoulder.

"Did you apply too?" he asked.

"Yeah, I did," I said while opening Instagram and searching for Meraki's page. My heart raced as I scrolled through the list.

But my name wasn't there.

I didn't get selected.

I stared at the screen, completely blank. I had missed my lectures to attend the recruitment stages, prepared so hard... and this was what I got.

Even those guys who didn't even care about social entrepreneurship had made it through — but I didn't.

A familiar person came behind me and saw the post opened up on my phone.

"Hey man! Are these the results? Let me check too," said someone as he grabbed my phone.

After a few seconds, he shouted joyfully, "YES! I'm selected. Woo-hoo!" He handed my phone back nonchalantly.

I couldn't take it anymore. Rage bubbled inside me.

I got up from my chair abruptly and stormed outside toward the main gate.

I heard Lokesh saying, "Wait, Ramit!" but I didn't stop.

I needed to get out of there.

I just walked away in anger, cursing the society heads who hadn't selected me. I sat in an auto rickshaw, heading toward Vishwavidyalaya Metro Station.

"Hello, Ramit. You look frustrated. All okay?"

I turned to see Samarth — the guy from the Meraki interview day.

Great. Another reminder of my failure. I gathered myself and tried to calm down. I forced a smile.

"Oh Hello Samarth. I'm doing fine, I guess. How are you?" I asked him.

"I'm doing great! Just got selected by Meraki. Did you see the results?" he asked, grinning.

I wanted to punch a wall.

But somehow, I kept my cool.

Everywhere I went, every person I stumbled upon was talking about this Meraki shit!

"Unfortunately, I didn't make it. But I'm happy for you. Congratulations," I said, keeping my voice as neutral as possible.

"Oh, that's sad. But you can always register for other societies. You can try your luck elsewhere and apply again. Thank you so much, though!" Samarth said, smiling.

The auto started moving. As we rode toward the station, we chatted a bit more about college life, professors, and different subjects.

Despite the circumstances, Samarth seemed like a genuinely good guy.

Maybe not all was lost yet.

7
Chapter Seven

Present Day – September 2031

"Where's my watch?" I asked.

"Did you check the wardrobe?" Mumma called back.

I went over to the almirah, opened it, and pulled out some drawers before finally finding my wristwatch packed neatly in a box. Pulling it out, along with one of my white shirts, I reminded myself of the importance of the day. An important meeting.

We were going to submit our documents to the government and concerned agencies - so that we could move forward with the licensing process. An essential step. A very important day.

"Did you gather all the documents?" Mumma asked.

"Yeah, I did. Just needed to cross-check once," I replied, struggling with my tie. Mumma noticed this and came toward me.

"All these years and you still struggle with a tie," she said, with a grin.

"Well, it is quite difficult to wear one in a single attempt. Such an elegant piece of clothing, yet so complicated to put on," I said as she helped me with it.

"There you go. A Double Windsor knot. Elegant, I must say," she smiled proudly.

"Classy. Thanks, Mumma," I said, looking in the mirror. "All set for today. I hope everything goes well."

"You'll be fine. I know it," she said reassuringly.

Samarth would be here soon. We were going to drive to the registry office together. I was anxious, but knowing that Samarth was by my side gave me confidence. We had gone through many ups and downs throughout our college days and since then. But we had always supported each other in miserable times, just like Xavi Hernandez and Andres Iniesta, assisting each other to reach our goals. I was so glad that we both clicked so well and decided to be partners in this venture.

The doorbell rang. I got up from my chair and opened the door, not surprised to find him standing there. It was Samarth, wearing a sharp black shirt with a pair of trousers of the same color.

"How do I look?" he asked, raising his hands and shrugging with a wide smile on his face.

"Dashing," I said, pulling him into a hug.

He greeted Mumma warmly, as I locked the gate behind him.

"How are you, Sam?" Mumma asked.

"Never been better," he laughed.

"Big day, huh?" he said, glancing at the documents neatly stacked and gathered on the table.

"Big day. For both of us," I replied. "I'll get you some tea, then we'll leave. You two catch up in the meantime."

I made my way to the kitchen, preparing tea while Mumma and Samarth chatted in the living room. Once I joined them, we talked about random things, laughing and easing the tension of the day ahead.

"So, shall we go?" I asked after finishing the last sip of my tea.

"Let's go," Sam said, getting up from the sofa.

We locked the door and walked to my car. It had been a while since I last sat behind the wheel. Taking God's name, we began the drive to the office, which wasn't far.

As we entered the parking lot, I received a call from Amit.

I picked it up.

"Good afternoon, sir. I've reached the office. Are you here yet?" he asked.

"Just parking my car. Will be there in five," I replied, steering my car into an empty slot and pulling the handbrake after putting the car into parking mode.

The three of us got out and made our way to the main gate of the office, where we found Amit waiting for us.

"I hope you brought all the documents?" he asked.

"Of course, Everything that was on your list," I said, showing him the bag of documents.

"Great. We'll go after three more slots. It will take around 35-40 minutes," Amit informed us.

We sat in the waiting hall until our turn came. Amit assisted us through the process, making everything a lot smoother. The government officials asked for documents and signatures on various forms. It took around two hours to complete everything.

At last, to wrap things up, one of the government officials told us that the status of the application would be notified in the upcoming days. They also gave us an application number and login credentials to track our progress on their website.

On our way back, Samarth and I brainstormed ideas to make our diner stand out. One idea we loved was hiring live musicians to perform every evening — it would create the perfect ambiance. I could already visualize it: light music floating through the air, people smiling, conversations flowing. It could become our USP.

I could literally visualize our place. A long journey to go, but when it would be done, I would be happy.

After dropping Samarth off, I went home, still buzzing with ideas. I immediately logged into the government registry website using the credentials they had given. It took a few minutes to load, but once it opened, seeing all the stages and our details laid out felt incredibly satisfying. Everything felt right.

Tonight, I was finally going to sleep well — after so long. The past few days had been exhausting but rewarding.

I surfed the internet for a while and glanced at the smart clock. The clock stood at 11 o'clock. I turned off the computer and canceled all the alarms for the morning, ready to rest, when a notification popped up on my phone. It was a text from Ayush.

"Hello Ramit. How are you? It's been a while. Can we meet someday? We've got a lot of things to catch up with."

A strange way to end the day as I was not expecting this text message. I thought he would never text after what had happened between us. But he did, and I was kind of surprised.

I stared at the notification, unsure how to respond. What do I say?

After thinking for a minute or two, I opened up the chat and typed:

"Hi Ayush. I'm doing fine. Yeah, sure. Absolutely. Do you have a place in mind?"

I clicked send. Within a second, he read it — almost as if he had been waiting.

His next message came almost immediately:

"I'm glad to know that you're doing well. I do have a place in mind. What about Delhi University North Campus? Where it all began. I want to start things with a fresh perspective. Same place, same people and a new start. You can say 'No,' but I hope you want to start things once again. Take your time to decide. Take the right choice, Ramit. Good night. Sleep Well."

Where it all began.

Vishwavidyalaya.

North Campus.

8
Chapter Eight

May 2023

It felt weird to be close friends with someone who wasn't even from my college. I hadn't been able to make friends within my own college. I could safely say that I had acquaintances—lots of them. Literally everyone, except for one or two. Except Samarth. He was from a different course too. Ironic.

I quickly searched up his contact number on the dialer app in my phone and tried calling him. He wasn't picking up. I tried calling Ayush too. But no response there either. I needed someone to talk to. I wanted to share things. Even though I was usually the person who listened to others, today I needed to talk to someone. I felt lost. I didn't really know how to make friends. I didn't know how to act normal when meeting new faces. College life felt pretty depressing.

I had a test the next day, and I hadn't even studied for it properly. It was a marketing subject test for internal assessment. I had to score well; otherwise, I might not achieve good grades in my first semester of college. Reviving my CGPA later would be a massive workload. I definitely needed to get back on track and work on my academic performance. Maybe I'd study early morning and just give it my best. I should probably go to sleep now.

As I covered myself with my blanket and closed my eyes, I drifted into a deep sleep almost instantly. It felt like I had slept for just two minutes when my alarm went off. I had slept well but not for long, I guess.

I studied for half an hour, did my daily morning chores, and got ready for the rest of my day quickly. I ate some biscuits with milk and bid farewell to Mumma.

"Keep yourself hydrated and eat something," she said as I stepped out. I nodded looking at her and started walking towards the Metro station. I had the notes saved with me on my phone; I'd revise for the test while traveling and everything would be fine. The weather was overcast today. Not quite sure if it would rain or not.

After reaching the station, I checked whether my Metro card had sufficient balance for the day's travel. I inserted the card into the card reader machine and it showed low balance. Great.

Now, I had to stand in a long queue to get my card recharged. The metro would arrive in two minutes and I was still stuck, standing there in the queue, waiting for it to move. If I caught this metro, I'd reach the college before the lectures started. If not, I'd be late.

I got ready to hand over the money and card to the man at the counter, quickly get to the AFC gate, climb up the stairs, and —if I were lucky—get inside the metro before the doors closed.

The queue moved along, and I quickly handed over the money and card to the man. He recharged my card in exactly seven seconds. Exactly seven seconds. Which now left me with approximately 35 seconds to get on the metro.

I brisk-walked to the AFC gates, scanning for the quickest one. All had a few people. I picked the one to the extreme right. I could hear the metro arriving on the platform. There was only one person in front of me, but his card wasn't working. He tapped it on the scanner, but the gate didn't open. I was losing time. Panic set in. I quickly shifted to the adjacent gate and tapped my card. I ran, two stairs at a time, trying to make it to the platform. The doors were closing. I was four steps away.

Should I jump in?

Probably not.

The doors closed.

"Oh, fucking great!" I muttered, watching the train pull away.

And then, I saw her.

She was standing just a few feet away, smiling as she watched the metro leave. There was something different about her smile—something calming.

For a moment, our eyes met briefly, and it felt like the frustration of missing the metro faded away in an instant. She was holding a book in her right hand, the strap of her bag in the other. Her hair, slightly out of place due to the rush, framed her face perfectly.

"Missed it too, huh?" she said, her voice so light, breaking the silence between us.

"Yeah," I replied, adjusting my bag slightly and giving a sheepish smile. "We're on the same boat now. Or, on the same platform." I joked, trying to read the minute details of her face. She chuckled softly.

"Part of life. It happens. There's always another one. Right?" she said.

"Yeah. Hopefully soon," I said, gazing at my wristwatch. "I don't want to be late."

She turned and sat on one of the platform seats, engrossed in her book. I couldn't help but look at her and smile.

To keep myself distracted, I pulled out my phone out of my pocket, only to see two missed calls from Ayush. Ugh, I had left my phone on silent once again. I didn't call back but texted him, saying that I'd call him in a while. Then I opened the calculator app, pretending to look busy in front of her. Then, I heard her gentle voice again.

"Sorry, but have I seen you before?" she asked, looking up. "You look familiar. Are you from Hindu College?"

No way.

"Yes! Department of Commerce. BMS 1st Year," I said a bit too enthusiastically. "Are you from Hindu too?"

"Yes! Department of Mathematics. B.Sc Mathematics Hons 1st Year," she said, smiling. "I knew I had seen you somewhere. You looked very upset that day."

Okay, now I remembered. She was probably talking about that Meraki results week. I had wandered here and there, feeling like a loser. I usually went to a deserted corner of the college to spend some time alone when I was sad.

I preferred cutting myself off from the world during low phases. She must have had seen me under a tree or something.

"Umm, hi? Are you okay?" she asked, noticing I had zoned out. Her voice registered in my ears, but I had been lost thinking about that week.

"Yeah. I zoned out for a bit. I think you saw me a few weeks ago, probably spending some time under the shade of a tree or something," I said.

"Now I remember. You were under that banyan tree, I guess. You looked sad. Is everything okay now?" she asked, visibly worried.

"Yeah, I'm doing better. Things weren't going great back then. Everyone I knew was getting selected for Meraki, the entrepreneurship society. I felt like a loser. Plus, other crappy stuff was going on. Part of life, I guess. Thanks for checking, though."

"Oh, damn. You had a lot on your mind. You need someone who'll listen to your problems. Sit here," she said, patting the seat next to her.

I was nervous, but her kind gesture made me feel comfortable. I sat beside her, bag on my lap.

"See, a lot of things happen in our lifetime. Okay, tell me one thing: was Meraki the last thing you wanted in life?"

"Absolutely not. I just wanted to do something great. Join a club or society. I guess I just wanted to be part of something. To do something big... like everyone else," I answered.

"Exactly. You said it yourself. See, it's not like being rejected means your life is over. No. I bet you're good at something. Maybe you weren't meant to be there. It happens. That's the beauty of life—you live it," she said.

"Well, that's... deep. And I guess you're right. Maybe I was being too pessimistic after all," I agreed with her.

The next metro arrived. We stood up and the conversation continued.

"By the way, I'm Mayanti. Mayanti Sinha. What's your good name?" she said, offering a handshake. I shook her hand, smiling. "Ramit Bansal. Nice to meet you."

Butterflies. God, why was I so nervous? I tried to stay cool but definitely failed. This is what happens when you have minimal interaction with girls. I envied guys who could stay cool.

We boarded the metro together but barely spoke. I wanted to talk more but didn't know how. I opened the PDF with my notes but couldn't focus. She was reading her Actuarial Science book. She seemed so smart, so focused. She struck me as a very studious and intellectual person.

We got off the metro and took the same rickshaw to college. When we reached, we stood there, awkwardly.

"It was nice meeting you, Ramit. Hope we meet again," she said, pulling a folded piece of paper from her jeans pocket. "Here's my contact number. If you ever feel sad, feel free to call or text."

My heart was thumping so fast. I didn't really know how to react. I took the piece of paper and held it tightly in my hand.

"Well, it was great meeting you. I'll drop a text later. Friends?" I said, offering my hand this time.

"Friends," she said, shaking it with a chuckle.

We both smiled at each other before heading in opposite directions.

I don't think this was our last meeting. Definitely not.

ᐯᐯᐯ

I reached my class a bit later than the reporting time. The professor told me to sit in the fourth row, on the third-last seat. He handed me the answer sheet and began writing the questions on the board. I wasn't well prepared, but somehow, I felt like I could still do well on the test. I answered all the questions to the best of my ability, elaborating with clear points wherever I could. I felt optimistic.

I felt good. Life felt good.

After classes got over, Lokesh ran up to me.

"Hi Ramit! How was your test today?"

"I wasn't fully prepared, but I gave it my best shot. What about you?" I asked.

"I messed up. I spent too much time on the first question and had to rush through the rest to finish it in time. Damn!" he said.

I placed a hand on his shoulder. "Hey, it was just a test, Lokesh. It carried only 20 marks, right?" He nodded.

"Twenty marks out of 160. That's around 12%—just twelve. Now, do you want to regret the 12% or focus on the remaining 88%? I'm sure the latter," I said.

"At least now you know that you need to work on your time management skills during exams. So, work on it. Improve. Evolve. Get better than you were yesterday," I added, trying to motivate and cheer him up.

He lifted his head, visibly more positive. Did I really cheer him up? It felt so good to help someone during a rough moment. Sometimes, all it takes is a little positivity to make life seem manageable again.

"You're right, Ramit. Thanks for cheering me up. I'll definitely work on improving myself. Wanna grab a sandwich?" he asked.

"Treats on me. Deal?" I said.

"Okay," he replied, and we both headed to the cafeteria.

What a great day.

9

Chapter Nine

Later That Day

"Yeah, I was kind of busy today. You know how it is—internal assessments, continuous evaluations, assignments and tests. I'm sorry I couldn't pick up your call," I said, pacing around the room while talking to Ayush on the phone.

"I'm sorry too. Hope you understand how packed things are these days. All the professors are just bombarding us with assignments and tests," Ayush replied, clearly frustrated.

"I know, right? And they expect us to attend every lecture, all the way till 4 or 5 P.M. By the time we get home, there's barely any time to breath before jumping into this mayhem. Aagghhh!" I said, venting out my frustration.

"Exactly. Anyway, that reminds me of the pending PPT I need to complete. I'll talk to you later. Hoping to meet soon. Bye, Ramit."

"Yeah, no worries. I'll sleep after a while too—need to give my body some rest. Catch you later. Good night," I said, and ended the call.

Finally, some peace. I could finally relax, especially after that test which had added so much weight to my already overloaded schedule. I lay down on my bed, and my eyes landed on the clothes hanging behind the door. I spotted my jeans—and then my wallet. That piece of paper from Mayanti!

I quickly jumped off the bed, grabbed my jeans, and pulled out the chit from my wallet. Fishing my phone from my pocket, I opened the Contacts app and saved her number as Mayanti Sinha.

Should I text her?

Or maybe not.

But I should.

I must.

I guess...

I opened up WhatsApp and began typing:

Hi Mayanti! Ramit this side. It was nice meeting you today. And I wanted to thank you for cheering me up.

I stared at the message for a good seven minutes before finally hitting send. As soon as I did, I tossed my phone aside and pretended to be busy.

Minutes later, the notification bell rang.

A message.

From Mayanti!

Hello there! I'm glad you texted. It was nice meeting you too.

After that, the conversation just... flowed.

Mayanti: Chalo, something good happened after we missed the damn train.

Ramit: Everything happens for a reason. If we hadn't missed the metro, we wouldn't be texting now.

Mayanti: So, what are you doing right now?

Ramit: Nothing much. What about you?

Mayanti: Just listening to music. Can't live without it...

Ramit: Wow! What kind of music do you like?

Mayanti: Nothing specific. I love good music—mostly Gen-X genres.

Ramit: I love Gen-X and Millennial music. Both Hindi and English! Similar tastes, I reckon... Who's your favourite Indian artist? Mine's KK.

Mayanti: I love KK! But I'm more of a Sonu Nigam fan. And Shreya Ghoshal is my loveeee!

Ramit: Shreya is definitely the best female singer out there. And Sonu? He's legendary! Looks like we really share similar music tastes!

We kept chatting for the next half an hour—talking about our favorite artists, college life, and random things in between.

The next day at college, there was a buzz around campus. Apparently, the college was offering a few additional courses, with classes held once or twice a week. Students were crowding around the notice boards, debating which courses to take.

I made my way to the board to check out the list. Tons of options were posted, but none of them sparked my interest— except one:

Understanding the Human Mind and Psychology — offered by the Department of Psychology.

Beneath the course description was a contact number. Without hesitation, I keyed it into my phone and stepped away from the crowd to make a call.

A calm voice answered, "Hello."

"Good afternoon, sir. Is this Professor Anand speaking? I saw your contact number on the notice board and wanted to inquire about your course," I said.

"Yes, this is Anand. Can you come meet me at the psychology department staff room?" he replied.

"Yes, sir! I'll be there in five minutes. Thank you!" I said, and hung up.

It took me a while to locate the staff room, with help of a few students and teachers. It was a mini-adventure in itself. The staff room, to my surprise, wasn't as spacious as the others. I knocked, asked for permission, and entered.

Inside sat a middle-aged man, probably in his 40s, wearing a crisp white shirt, blue trousers, and polished black shoes. He was scribbling something in a diary when I walked in.

"Good afternoon, sir. I'm Ramit Bansal from the Department of Commerce. I called earlier about your course," I said.

He smiled warmly. "Ah, yes. You're the first one to call today. Not many students show interest in this field—God knows why. I'm Anand, and I teach psychology. This course explores how the human mind works, how one can become emotionally strong and intelligent, and much more. Classes will begin in a week or two and continue until graduation. It's for those who are genuinely interested."

He explained everything with such calmness and clarity— A refreshing contrast to the usual uptight professors.

"I actually studied psychology in high school and loved the subject, I'll definitely consider joining. I'm looking forward to your classes. Thank you for taking the time, sir," I said.

He gave a small, encouraging smile as I left.

Outside, it struck me—maybe his small reflected how little attention this subject received. Mainstream choices always hogged the spotlight. But now, I was beginning to understand.

I hope he gets a bigger staff room someday. Psychology is a wonderful field. It has always fascinated me. Even in high school, I had a deep interest in it, while most of my peers stuck to the typical subjects.

I'm definitely going to choose this one. I'm pretty sure that it will add value to my life. After all, who wouldn't want to be emotionally intelligent and strong? Man is a social animal, and relationships demand maturity and self-awareness.

I headed straight to the admin department, grabbed the add-on course form, and walked over to my usual spot for filling it out—the banyan tree.

As I was scribbling away, I noticed a familiar figure approaching. I assumed she was just passing by, so I kept writing.

Then, a shadow loomed over me.

I looked up.

It was Mayanti!

"Is this your 'escape from reality' place?" she teased with a laugh.

I laughed back. "Might just be. I'm filling out the add-on course form. Are you applying for one too?"

"Umm, I'm gonna pass," she said after a thoughtful pause.

"Why?" I asked, curious. "There are so many options—and it's free!"

She sat down beside me in the shade and explained, "I'm planning to prepare for some competitive exams during college. I want to stay focused. An Add-on course would just be a distraction. Hope you get my point."

"I see. What kind of exams, if you don't mind sharing?"

"I'm not fully sure yet… but maybe something in actuarial science or statistics. I love playing with numbers, stats, and data. Or maybe even apply for graduate programs abroad," she said.

"That's nice. I get it—big dreams," I said, returning to my form.

"So, which subject are you choosing?" she asked, peeking at my form.

"Understanding The Human Mind and Psychology. I'm really into it. Always wanted to learn more."

"Wow. Psychologist Ramit Bansal… sounds weird!" she joked, bursting into laughter.

I smiled. "Well, it's lecture time. I'll take your leave. See you soon. Bye!" she said, shaking my hand before walking toward the campus building.

I waved back and headed to the administration office to submit the completed form.

The staff there told me that the course allotment would be on a first-come, first-serve basis.

As if a bazillion students were lining up for psychology.

I'll definitely get in.

Thus ended my day at college—new subject, new conversations, productive classes, and a little more excitement added to my regular routine.

A good day indeed.

10
Chapter Ten

2 Weeks Later – June 2023

"So, my name is Anand Krishnan. I completed my bachelor's in Psychology from Kirori Mal College and pursued my master's abroad, in London. I came back to India in 2015 to pursue a career in teaching. I joined Delhi University in 2016, and ever since then, I have been teaching in different colleges of DU. I came here to Hindu back in 2019," Professor Anand introduced himself. "Well, that's pretty much about me. Now, I would like you all to introduce yourselves," he said to the class, which consisted of only twelve students, including me.

All the students started introducing themselves, talking about their hobbies and career plans. My turn was approaching, and I found myself rehearsing what to say in my mind. It felt weird—after all, who rehearses a formal introduction beforehand? It's just a few basic details. Still, I stood up and said, "Hello everyone. Good morning, sir. I am Ramit Bansal. I like to read and write, and I also love listening to music. I am currently pursuing my BMS degree from this college and will probably work in the corporate sector in the future." I sat down quickly. The other students introduced themselves too; we were all from different courses. I didn't know a single person in that room.

Anand sir taught us the basics of psychology that day. We learned about Sigmund Freud, Hans Selye, and other important figures in this field of study. He taught calmly and patiently, with such composure. I had seen professors who were so blunt and strict, even in the very first introductory lecture. But Anand sir was different. He was very soft-spoken and composed throughout.

I had been trying hard to attend all my lectures these days. Some days, I felt confident about my attendance; other days, it felt like there was still a long way to go. I had missed a few days in April, dealing with backlogs.

It was tough, but I was hopeful that I'd get through this. I had made a few acquaintances at least—not many I would call close friends, though.

My routine these days was pretty fixed: 8 to 3 college, 3 to 4 travel, 4 to 12 rest, study, and whatever else came up. And then the cycle repeated. Day after day. Night after night.

It was currently 2 PM and I didn't have any lectures left. There was a fest going on at the college. Honestly, it felt like there was a fest every other day, but I usually skipped them unless I was free. Today was one of those rare free days. This fest, organized by the Linguistics Society, was called *Linguistics-Mania*. A weird name, to be honest. They could have seriously come up with a better name. You'd expect better from a society devoted to language.

There were different stalls: games, quizzes, food. I wandered around, here and there, looking at them casually until one stall caught my interest. It was a geography and language game. Behind each pluck card was a city's name, and you had to name the language spoken there. If you named 8 out of 10 correctly, you'd win a prize. I watched a few participants struggle; the best performance so far was 7 correct answers.

I wasn't quite sure if I should try it, when suddenly, I felt someone poke my arm. I turned around—and there she was. Mayanti.

We always seemed to bump into each other.

She looked really happy. Waving at me, she asked, "Hello once again! What are you doing here?"

"Nothing much. Just checking out the stalls. What about you?" I replied.

"Just wandering around. What is this game?" she asked, stepping closer. Before I could explain, the society volunteers did. "I want to try it," she said excitedly.

I watched as she played. The round started, along with the stopwatch, and one by one, she answered each and every question correctly. She got one right, then another, and then one more. Correct, correct, correct.

She didn't even miss a single pluck card and answered all the cards correctly—a perfect 10 out of 10. The crowd cheered for her. I stood there, awestruck. How could someone even know this many languages? Who even knows which language is spoken in Luxembourg? (It's French, by the way.) But she knew.

The Linguistics Society hyped her up, and she jumped with happiness. And then, something completely unexpected happened.

She turned, looked at me—and hugged me tightly.

It lasted just two seconds before she pulled away, realizing what she'd done. She gave me a sheepish smile. "Sorry. Got a bit carried away."

"It's okay," I said, trying to process what had just happened. I was trembling, to be honest. A girl had never hugged me before. Never in my entire life. Never.

I awkwardly clapped along with the others, avoiding her gaze.

They gave her a luxury-brand chocolate as a prize. We walked away from the crowd, and I tried starting a conversation. "That was amazing, what you did back there. How do you know so much about languages?"

She smiled, looking at the chocolate. "I have always wanted to travel and study abroad. I've done a lot of research on different countries and universities. I guess that's why I know so much about languages."

"That's incredible," I said.

She unwrapped the chocolate and offered me half. I hesitated. "Are you sure?" I asked.

She nodded. "Of course. I want to share it with you."

I couldn't say no to that face. "Thank you so much," I said, accepting it.

"It's really good," I said after a bite.

She agreed.

"So, do you have any lectures right now?" she asked me, tossing the chocolate wrapper in a nearby bin.

"Nope. Done for the day."

"Me too," she said.

Since we lived in the same locality, we decided to travel home together.

At the metro station, we talked about life.

"How's life treating you?" she asked.

"Well, I don't really know. Feels like a low phase. What about you?" I replied.

"To be very honest, life's okay, but it could be better," she said.

Why is it always it could be better? Why is it never I'm satisfied? Everyone seemed so stressed these days.

"I believe th—" I paused because she started to say something too.

"You were saying?" she prompted.

I continued, "I think this is a transitioning phase. That's why it feels so overwhelming. It'll get better with time."

The metro arrived. We boarded, found seats easily (for once—it wasn't crowded).

"Yes, I totally agree with you," she said. "It must get better. Otherwise... I don't know what'll happen to all of us."

"Yeah... Exams are next month. It feels like yesterday was our first day of college. Time really flies. It really does," I said, resting my head back.

She stayed silent for a few minutes, then said, "Isn't it weird? When we want life to slow down a bit, it speeds up. When we want it to speed up, it drags. Especially during tough and miserable times."

She looked at her wristwatch.

I looked at mine too, then showed it to her. "That's the beauty of it. That's the whole point. This circle of life keeps on moving. We can't stop it. All we can do is move along with it. And when it's time, it will stop ticking—for good. Just like our lives. We have one life. Gotta live it up." I stopped my watch to symbolize it.

She smiled at me—a genuine, hopeful smile.

"Symbolism at its peak. You talk like a writer or poet sometimes," she said.

"Well, I am something of a writer myself," I laughed.

"For real? What do you write?"

"I love writing. Poems, stories, essays, monologues. Anything. I can write all day long, really."

"I would love to read your work someday," she said excitedly.

"Someday, I'll share it," I replied.

We had a wholesome conversation throughout the journey. We talked about various things, unlike our last trip in the metro together, when we sat in silence. This time, it felt natural. Comfortable. Like we were slowly growing into something more.

After about an hour, we reached our station. We had to exit through different gates.

"That was a good talk. We should do it more often," I said.

"Yes, of course," she replied.

We shook hands and waved goodbye.

Once again, we walked in opposite directions.

I didn't want the conversation to end. I liked being around her. It was comfortable.

Am I falling in love?

Am I?

11

Chapter Eleven

Present Day

As I walked through the bustling streets of Vishwavidyalaya, memories flooded back. This was where it had all began—where dreams soared high against the backdrop of Northern Delhi. Where we used to sit and discuss our careers, believing we had it all figured out.

I couldn't help but smile at how naïve we were back then.

So many memories were attached to this place.

"You're early," Ayush's voice pulled me from my thoughts. I turned to see him grinning, that same old spark in his eyes.

"I guess I just wanted to soak it all in—all the memories flooding back," I said, glancing around.

"It hasn't changed much, right?" Ayush asked.

"Not much," I replied, pausing for a moment before completing my thought. "But we have."

He looked at me and smiled, though there was pain in his eyes. I could see it.

As Tony Montana once said, *"The eyes, Chico. They never lie."*

We settled into one of our favourite old cafes and ordered some sandwiches.

For a moment, it felt like we were back in our college days.

But there was a weight in our conversation now, a depth that hadn't existed back then.

"So, how's the restaurant idea going?" he asked, leaning back in his chair.

I was surprised. How did he know about that? I had never mentioned it—at least, I didn't think I had.

"Wait, what? How do you know? Who told you?" I asked, leaning forward, resting my hands on the table.

"Well, I have my sources. Did my homework," he said, taking a sip of water.

"Oh, come on! Tell me. Who told you?" I pressed.

"I can't reveal my credible sources," he said with a grin. "But I can tell you it was someone we both know. That's all you're getting—at least for now."

"Woah... That's surprising. But trust me, Ayush, I will find out who it was," I said, leaning back in my chair.

"You have not changed, have you?" he said, bursting out in laughter. I sat there, visibly confused.

"Aunty told me about it. When we last met, in the metro. Remember?"

How could I even forget that? Of course Mumma told him about the restaurant that night.

"After all these years, you still forget things? You haven't changed much, really," he chuckled.

I shrugged.

I hesitated, then continued, "It's coming together. Slowly, gradually. Sometimes, I have self-doubts about whether I'm capable of running a business like this. But I'm trying to do my best."

Ayush nodded thoughtfully. "You haven't changed much either. I always admired your passion—how you throw yourself into what excites you."

I smiled, looking at him warmly.

"Where's the location, by the way?" he asked.

"Wait, didn't your 'source' tell you that too? I'm astonished," I teased.

He laughed and shook his head. "It is what it is," he said, pressing for an answer again.

"Well, it's not too far from here—Central Delhi, Connaught Place," I told him.

"Wow! That's great. I love that place. I like to call it the heart of Delhi."

I smiled, realizing I had never thought of it that way before, but he was right—it really did feel like *the heart of Delhi.*

"I have applied for licensing and the rest of the formalities. Let's see how it goes," I added.

"That's a great start, actually. You've laid the cornerstone. Things will fall into place. Trust the process," he said reassuringly.

"So, how about you? How's life?" I asked, genuinely curious.

He scoffed lightly and stayed silent for a moment, as if searching for the right words.

"Well... I don't know," he finally said.

"What? What do you mean you don't know?" I asked.

"The world has changed," he replied.

"You remember how I always said I'd become an accountant?"

"Yes, I remember," I said.

"Well, I did it. Graduated from Hansraj, got a placement offer at one of the biggest corporate firms. Thought it would make life easier. I joined right after graduation," he paused, his eyes dropping to the table.

"And then?" I urged gently, placing a hand on his shoulder. "Hey? You okay?"

"Yeah, I'm fine," he said.

"Where was I? Right—Accountant at the firm.

I didn't hate the work, but I didn't love it either. I thought it was my purpose. I worked there for two years. But they were tough years."

"What happened?" I asked, concerned.

"I was climbing the ranks quickly, giving it my all. I had a stable career. But then there was this major client—one of the firm's biggest—ran into huge financial trouble. I was put on a team of other accountants, tasked with 'adjusting' their financial statements. Making things look better than they really were.

My supervisor was all up for it, said it was just 'how this game was played.'"

"That's messed up," I said, feeling a surge of anger on his behalf.

"They made it clear that if I refused, it could cost me my job—or worse, my entire career. But if I went along... I could've ended up on the wrong side of the law. I couldn't do it."

"And you left?" I asked him, now understanding why he'd leave such a stable path.

"Yeah," Ayush nodded. "It wasn't worth selling my integrity. I'd rather start over from scratch than live my life looking over my shoulder, wondering when it would all come crashing down."

"You made the right decision," I said firmly.

"I think so. Even though it was very hard at the time. Looking back, it was worth it," he said.

"I mean, if you are happier now, then of course it was worth it," I said, just as the waiter arrived with our order. We thanked him and started eating.

Ayush continued, opening a ketchup packet.

"The months after that were tough. I had no job, no clear direction. I was miserable, not able to understand where I should go next," he said.

"But I was determined to get back on track, to rebuild. I decided to pivot—started learning about investment banking. I could have easily entered this field with my degree, but it made more sense to go for an MBA."

"Oh, that means that you—

"I did my MBA first," he said proudly, cutting me off. "Cleared CAT on my first attempt. Got into one of the best IIMs."

"Which one?" I asked excitedly.

"Ahmedabad," he said, leaning back in his chair with a proud smile.

"Completed my MBA, worked at a brokerage firm as an investment banker for a while, gathered experience, and when the time felt right, I started my own firm," he finished.

"That's honestly inspirational. I'm really happy for you," I said, meaning every word.

We continued chatting about life and other random topics.

Time flew by, and soon it was time to ask for the bill.

When it came, I suggested splitting it.

But Ayush smiled and said, "My treat. Enough said."

He paid the entire bill before I could protest.

"This isn't fair, Ayush," I said, raising an eyebrow.

"We met after so long. I owed you a treat before... well, before anything. That's why," he said with a grin.

"But next time, I am paying. No 'ifs' and 'buts,'" I warned.

He laughed as we walked out of the café.

"Well, we still have a lot of catching up to do," he said.

"How about meeting every week? Same day, same time, same place?"

I thought for a moment.

"I mean, yeah... we can do that," I agreed.

"It was nice meeting you, Ramit, after so long. So every Friday, 7 PM, right here?"

"Done deal," I said, extending my hand for a handshake.

"Deal," he replied, shaking my hand with a laugh.

It was a moment of parting—but not for long.

At least, I hoped not.

12

Chapter Twelve

June 2023

Semester-end examinations were less than two weeks away, and honestly, I didn't feel confident at all. There was just so much to study, and I still had a mountain of backlogs to clear. The fact that these were going to be our very first college examinations made me all the more anxious. What should be the word limit for answers? What was the right way to present them? A million questions were buzzed through my head.

There were some teachers and "guides" on the internet, but they didn't seem very experienced. I really felt there should have been a proper handbook or at least a mentor dedicated to university examinations. Some professors were truly helpful, but some were the complete opposite — and honestly, I hated dealing with teachers like that.

The good part? I had managed to make some great friends who were equally willing to help everyone pass this examination season without losing their minds. With them by my side, I felt a little more reassured.

"How's the prep going?" Mumma asked, walking into my room with a steaming cup of coffee.

"It's fine, to be honest. Could be better," I said, taking the cup and placing it on my desk.

"Make sure to rest too. Don't strain yourself," she said gently, planting a kiss on my cheek. "Don't stay up for long. Sleep before midnight, okay?" she added before leaving.

I had a goal: finish at least three topics that night. I opened up the lesson on my laptop, pen and notebook ready, sipping coffee as the lecture played. For the next hour and a half, I stayed glued to the screen, trying to absorb as much as I could.

Then I tried to make notes — jotting down the topics. But somewhere along the way, it all fell apart. I found myself staring blankly at the same page, the words blurring together. No matter how hard I tried, the lines of text refused to stick. I glanced at the clock—**11:05 PM**. I should've been halfway through by then.

But every time I started to make sense of the content, her face would appear in my mind, unbidden — **Mayanti**.

The way her hair fell softly across her shoulders, the way her smile lit up her face when she caught me staring at her... I shook my head, trying to dispel the thoughts, but they lingered persistently.

I focused my eyes back on the notebook, determined to concentrate. "Focus," I muttered to myself, trying to read through the paragraphs. But all I could think about was the way her eyes crinkled when she smiled. The sound of her voice — how it echoed in my brain, on repeat.

"Ridiculous," I said aloud, leaning back in my chair, closing my eyes, trying to reset my thoughts and focus on my studies. As I closed my eyelids, all I could see was her beautiful face. All I could see was her, walking right by my side on the campus, her voice echoing in my mind. Her voice, sweet and gentle — I could hear it.

I glanced at my phone, tempted to text her. But what would I even say? *'Hey, can't stop thinking about you'?* No, that would be weird. But the urge to talk to her, to hear her voice, was overwhelming. I grabbed my phone, scrolled through our brief conversation from the other day, frustration mounting, before setting the phone down again.

Why was this happening now?

I forced myself to focus on my notebook once again, trying to build some concentration. "Come on! Focus!" I muttered, picking up the pen.

The harder I tried, the more vivid my thoughts became. Struggling to focus on my studies, I gave up and closed my notes. Not a productive day.

Maybe tomorrow would be better.

This had never happened to me before. I could remember every tiny detail about her — how she smiled, how she looked down shyly when she laughed. These small intricate details. I remembered them as if they were imprinted on the lobes of my brain.

Realizing I wasn't going to get any studying done that night, I closed the book with a sigh. Maybe tomorrow I'd have better luck. But as I turned off the light and lay down in bed, I knew she'd be the last thing I thought of before I drifted off to sleep.

The alarm blared from my phone, snapping me awake.

That day was the last day of our first semester — after this, it would be nothing but preparatory leave and exams for the next few months.

The past few days had flown by. Hard to believe that already, one-sixth of my college life was over.

I dragged myself through the usual boring morning routine and headed to college to submit my final assignments. The campus felt deserted — not surprising, considering everyone had unofficially begun their study leave.

Assignments submitted, assessments completed. Finally... now it was time to fully focus on exam preparations.

Except, I could barely focus last night.

Some days at college just felt *empty*. After six months, I realized something very clearly — college without friends was unbearable. I couldn't even imagine how those without any friends got through their days. It must have been soul-crushing.

I had truly understood that there was absolutely no way you could survive college, without friends.

I never wanted to experience that. **Ever.**

I was about to leave when my phone rang.

It was **Ayush Malhotra** — the guy from Hansraj.

"Hello?" I answered.

"Hey Ramit, are you still around North Campus?"

"Yeah, just about to head home. Boring day. What about you?"

"Well, college's empty, and my friends aren't around either. Thought maybe we could go out and chill before exam madness begins. You in?" he asked.

I glanced at my watch.

"Umm... yeah, sure. Where do we meet?"

"Vishwavidyalaya metro station. I was thinking, let's head to a café in CP. What do you say?"

"Sounds good. I'll be there in five. I'll call you when I reach," I said, stepping out to find an auto-rickshaw.

Even the autos were scarce that day.

The ride to Vishwavidyalaya was quiet.

I felt a slight pang of guilt about going out instead of studying — but hey, it was our first semester. Got to live a little, right?

When I reached the station, I spotted Ayush waiting at a distance. I quickened my pace and greeted him warmly. It had been almost 45 days since we last met in person, but we had stayed connected through social media and calls.

"Hey there! How's it going?" I said, shaking his hand firmly.

"I'm good! You?"

"All good. Shall we?" Ayush clapped me on the shoulder — an easy gesture that immediately made me feel at ease.

"Ready to explore CP?" he asked.

I grinned. "Yeah. I've heard a lot about it but never really *explored* it."

"Perfect. It's a North Campus rite of passage," Ayush laughed as we hopped onto the metro.

The ride was smooth, and conversation flowed easily. We talked about professors, classes, first impressions of our respective colleges. Despite not spending much time together during the semester, there was a natural camaraderie growing between us.

"So, why did you choose Hindu?" Ayush asked as we neared Rajiv Chowk.

I shrugged. "Good reputation. Plus, family pressure."

Ayush chuckled. "Ah, the family push. I get it. Hansraj wasn't my first choice either. But it grows on you."

Our conversation meandered between subjects, flowing with the ease of two people who were slowly getting to know each other. The distance between Vishwavidyalaya and Rajiv Chowk flew by, and soon, we reached the destination. Connaught Place, CP. *The heart of Delhi.*

As we stepped out onto the bustling platform at Rajiv Chowk, the energy of Connaught Place hit us immediately. The crowd, the traffic, the overwhelming number of shops and restaurants — it was nothing like the relatively peaceful confines of North Campus.

"Welcome to the chaos," Ayush said with a grin. "Let's head to a café I know. Best cold coffee you'll ever have, trust me."

I followed Ayush through the crowded streets of CP, dodging pedestrians and rickshaws as we made our way towards the café. It was a small place, tucked between larger, more modern buildings, with a rustic charm that seemed to belong to a different era. As we stepped inside, the atmosphere immediately felt different — calm, quiet, with the aroma of fresh coffee filling the air.

"This place is a hidden gem," Ayush said, leading me to a table by the window.

I took a seat, glancing around. The café was simple — wooden tables, cozy lighting, and the low hum of quiet conversation in the background. It wasn't the most luxurious place, but it had a charm I couldn't quite put into words.

As we settled in and ordered our drinks, the conversation drifted to bigger topics — hopes, ambitions, and the future.

I found myself opening up more than I usually did, sharing my uncertainties about college, career plans, and much more.

"That's actually pretty cool," Ayush said, sipping his iced coffee. "You've got the whole plan in your head already?"

"Not really," I said. "I mean, I have a few ideas, but I'm scared of messing up."

Ayush leaned back in his chair, nodding thoughtfully. "Everyone feels like that, man. You think I have it all figured out? I barely know what I want to do with my life after college. But you've got passion, and that's already more than most people."

I smiled, feeling a little more at ease. Ayush had a way of making things sound simple, even when they weren't.

"So what about you?" I asked. "What's your plan after graduation?"

Ayush paused for a moment, glancing out the window as if searching for the answer in the crowded streets of CP. "I don't know yet," he said softly. "My parents want me to go into accounting or finance — something stable, you know? But honestly, I'm not sure if that's what I want. I've been thinking about taking some time off after college, maybe traveling, figuring things out."

I nodded. "That sounds nice. I wish I had the guts to do something like that."

"You could, you know," Ayush said, leaning forward. "You don't have to follow anyone else's script. Write your own. Do what makes you happy."

Our conversation flowed easily from that point, with Ayush recounting stories of his childhood trips to CP and me sharing my experiences at Hindu.

The hours seemed to pass by in a blur, and before we knew it, the sun had begun to set, casting long shadows across the streets outside the café. As we stepped out of the café, I hadn't expected this — this connection with Ayush, this easy camaraderie — but it felt right.

"Thanks for today," I said as we walked toward the metro station. "I didn't realize how much I needed this."

Ayush smiled, clapping me on the back. "Anytime, man. We've got to do this more often. North Campus can get suffocating after a while."

As we boarded the metro back to our homes, the train was quieter than it had been earlier in the day. I leaned back in my seat, reflecting on the day's events. Ayush wasn't just a casual acquaintance anymore — he was someone I felt I could truly connect with. And though neither of us had all the answers, it didn't seem to matter.

Our bond, formed over shared cups of coffee and conversation, was enough for now.

13

Chapter Thirteen

October 2023

October had always been a peculiar month. A season of transition, a time when the chaos of summer slowly faded, giving way to a more introspective autumn. In Delhi, the month brought with it the subtle shift from unbearable heat to a cool breeze — the kind of breeze that made you want to stay outside just a little longer, to breathe in the air just a little deeper. Except for the part where the smog and pollution began to creep in.

And yet, as I stood at the gates of my college, staring at the campus that had once felt like a sanctuary, I realized that this October was different.

We were officially back for the second semester. The June—September exams were over, the endless hours of cramming and sleepless nights were behind us. But the relief I thought I'd feel after our long break never really came. Instead, there was a restlessness growing inside me, something I couldn't quite place. And, like most things these days, it had to do with Mayanti.

It wasn't supposed to be like this. I wasn't supposed to feel this way.

The last few months had been a blur of confusion, and every time I thought I had a handle on my feelings, Mayanti would appear—smiling that infectious smile of hers—and everything I thought I knew would unravel.

It had been nearly three months since I last saw her. Three weeks since our exams had ended and she had left for home. We kept in touch, of course—texts, late-night chats, the occasional phone call—but nothing felt the same. I tried to focus on myself, to get my head straight, but she was always there, lingering at the back of my mind.

And now, she was back.

I hadn't seen her yet, but I knew it was only a matter of time—college had started again, and like gravity, we would inevitably be pulled back into each other's orbit. The thought both thrilled and terrified me.

I slung my bag over my shoulder and walked toward the campus, weaving through the familiar crowds. The air buzzed with the excitement of a new semester—old friends reuniting, the unspoken promise of a fresh start. But for me, it felt like stepping into something far more complicated.

It felt like the first day of college all over again. Anxiety and nervousness kicked in, but everything felt... different. There were old faces around, but with new masks. In time, I had changed too—just enough to notice. A sense of seniority ran through me; I thought it would make things easier, that I could navigate college life better now. But I couldn't. The reason being Mayanti, once again.

I wandered around the campus—a restless wanderer searching for something. Or someone.

And then, I found her.

Near the canteen, sitting at one of the outdoor tables with a group of friends. She was laughing, her head thrown back, the sunlight catching the edges of her hair, turning it almost golden. For a moment, I froze, my feet refusing to move. There she was—as beautiful and carefree as ever—completely unaware of the storm brewing inside me.

I forced myself forward, hoping that my face wouldn't betray the emotions swirling in my chest. As I approached, she looked up and saw me. Her smile widened instantly, and for a brief second, everything else disappeared.

"Hi Ramit!" she called out, waving. "It's been a while!"

I grinned, trying to keep my voice casual. "Yeah, it feels like it."

She stood up, and before I could react, she had wrapped her arms around me in a quick hug. It was nothing out of the ordinary—just a friendly gesture—but my heart hammered in my chest all the same. I hugged her back briefly, inhaling the faint scent of her perfume, and for a split second, I allowed myself to enjoy the closeness before pulling away.

"How was the break?" she asked, sitting back down and gesturing for me to join her.

"It was good," I lied, sliding into the chair. "Yours?"

"Not bad," she replied, brushing a strand of hair behind her ear. "But I'm glad to be back. I missed everyone."

Everyone. That was the thing about Mayanti—she had a way of making everyone feel like they mattered, like they were important to her. And maybe that was why I felt like this—why I couldn't shake these feelings, no matter how hard I tried.

We talked for a while—about classes, professors, all the usual stuff. But underneath it all, there was something else, something unspoken hanging between us. Every time she laughed, every time our eyes met, I felt it. And I wondered if she did too.

Eventually, it was time for my lectures. I left her after a few reluctant minutes, telling myself it was the right thing to do. But as the days passed, my affection for her only grew stronger.

Day by day.
Moment by moment.
And there was nothing I could do to stop it.

I had never felt like this before. Not once in my life. This was the first time.

It wasn't until later that day, sitting together in the library, that the weight of it all finally crashed down on me. We had a long gap between classes and decided to get some studying done, though in reality, neither of us was paying much attention to the books in front of us.

Mayanti was sitting across from me, flipping through her notes, her brow furrowed in concentration. I was supposed to be reading, but all I could think about was her—how her lips pursed slightly when she was focused, how her fingers tapped rhythmically on the edge of the table, how her presence seemed to fill the entire room.

And that's when it happened. The realization that I had been avoiding for months finally settled in.

I was falling for her.

I stared at her, my heart pounding, and for a brief moment, everything seemed to freeze. The sounds of the library faded away, the movement of students around us became a blur, and all I could focus on was her. It wasn't just her laugh, or her smile, or the way she made me feel at ease. It was everything—her kindness, her strength, the way she saw the world with such clarity and conviction.

I had never felt this way about anyone before, and it scared me. Because once you fall for someone—really fall—there's no going back. You can't un-feel it. And I wasn't sure I was ready for that.

I blinked, trying to shake the thoughts from my head. I couldn't let this happen. Not now. We had our futures to think about. College, careers, life.

But it was too late.

The feelings were already there. Whether I wanted them or not.

14

Chapter Fourteen

6ᵗʰ November 2023

Later that evening, after our classes had ended, Mayanti and I walked to the metro station together. It had become our routine during the first semester—walking to the station, catching the metro, talking about anything and everything. It was one of the things I had missed the most over the break.

As we approached the platform, she nudged me with her elbow.

"Hey, I was thinking... maybe we could grab coffee sometime this week? You know, just to catch up properly."

I raised an eyebrow, trying to play it cool. "Sure, sounds good. When?"

"How about tomorrow? There's this new café near Dilli Haat that I've been dying to try."

I nodded, my mind already racing. Coffee. Just the two of us. It wasn't a date—at least, not officially—but the thought of spending time with her outside of college, away from the usual group of friends, made my heart race.

"Tomorrow it is," I said, trying to keep my voice steady.

She smiled, and for a moment, everything felt right. But as we boarded the metro and the train began to move, I couldn't shake the feeling that things were about to change.

I didn't know if it would be for the better or worse, but one thing was certain—I was falling for her, and there was no turning back.

I couldn't sleep that night. At least, not before 2 A.M. All I could think of was her. It seemed like I was long gone — I had fallen for her so hard that I might never get back up. Oh, to be in love — it's the best feeling in this world, but it can just as easily be the worst.

The next day arrived faster than I had anticipated. I spent the entire morning restless, unable to focus on anything. The thought of seeing Mayanti outside of college, sitting across from her in a cozy café, made my stomach twist into knots.

When I arrived at the café near Dilli Haat, she was already there, sitting at a table by the window. She waved when she saw me, and I made my way over, trying to steady the nervous energy buzzing inside me.

"Hey," she said as I sat down. "I ordered for both of us. Hope you don't mind."

I smiled. "Not at all."

We talked about everything and nothing—about classes, the latest movies we had watched, about our plans for the semester. But underneath the casual conversation, there was an unspoken tension, a current of emotions that neither of us could ignore. It was difficult to meet her gaze directly. Whenever her eyes locked onto mine, I could barely hold it for more than three seconds, no matter how hard I tried.

At one point, she leaned forward, resting her chin on her hand.

"You seem different," she said softly.

I blinked, caught off guard. "Different? How?"

"I don't know," she said, her eyes searching mine. "You've just been... quieter lately. Like there's something on your mind."

I swallowed hard, unsure of how to respond. There was something on my mind, but I couldn't tell her. Not yet.

"I've just been thinking a lot," I said, aiming for casual.

"About what?" she asked, her voice soft, almost hesitant.

I hesitated, my heart pounding. This was it. This was the moment. I could tell her everything — lay my feelings bare — or I could bury it all and pretend.

But as I looked into her eyes, I knew there was no moving on from her.

"You know, I keep overthinking stuff… random things. It is what it is."

I lied.

I couldn't afford to tell her how I felt. Not yet. There was too much at stake, and I couldn't bear to risk the friendship — or the inevitable awkwardness that could follow.

She reached out and rested her hand on mine. My heart lurched, pounding so violently it felt like it might break free from my chest.

"Hey. If there's anything you need to talk about, you know I'm always here, right?" she said, her voice so gentle it nearly broke me.

"Yes, of course, Mayanti. I know."

I tried to anchor myself, to hold back the words I so badly wanted to say.

If only she knew—

She was the storm I couldn't escape.

What a strange dilemma love is.

How do you express your feelings when everything else demands your focus?

Months slipped by like a swift breeze. And once again, it was exam season.

This time, it felt like it had come around even faster.

Our second semester was drawing to a close, marking the end of our first year of college.

Almost one-third of our college life, gone.

I could hardly believe it.

I hadn't scored great grades last semester—not terrible, but not what I knew I was capable of.

This time was different.

I had attended lectures properly, made good notes, stuck to a study schedule.

This time, I was ready. I wasn't going to hold back.

It was time to step up. To prove it to myself—and to those who had doubted me.

Only one obstacle stood between me and my goal: her.
   She was both my catalyst and my impediment.

Who would have thought?
   We still talked, occasionally.

But for now, I had been trying to distance myself—focus on the bigger things happening around me.
And yet, no matter how far I tried to pull away, she was always there.

Always lingering, just at the edge of every thought.

15
Chapter Fifteen

Present Day – October 2031

I stood in the middle of my living room, hands on my hips, taking in everything I'd set up. The table was already set, a neat row of plates and silverware gleaming under the soft glow of the lights. The food was still in the kitchen, resting under foil to keep warm. It all looked good—perfect, almost—but something still felt off.

I adjusted one of the cushions on the sofa, though it didn't need it. I'd done this a dozen times already, but my nerves wouldn't let me relax. Inviting Ayush over for dinner had seemed like a good idea at the time — a way to maybe bridge the growing gap between us. Now, as the minutes ticked by, I wasn't so sure.

I stopped fussing with the cushions and crossed to the window, looking out at the darkening sky. The city outside was alive, as it always was, but inside this apartment, it felt like time crawled. A cool October breeze drifted in through the open window, carrying with it the faint scent of smoke from nearby Diwali preparations. I could see the glow of fairy lights from neighbouring buildings, reminding me of how the festive season always felt lighter, happier, back when things were different.

I let out a breath, my fingers tapping against the windowsill. It hadn't always been this tense between us. There used to be an ease. It felt like there was an invisible wall between us now—one that neither of us was sure how to climb over.

I couldn't help but think of all the times we'd been in sync, especially in college. Vishwavidyalaya, CP, those late nights brainstorming plans for the future—for a life we thought we had figured out. The kind of friendship where you didn't need to explain things; you just got each other. But those days felt distant now, like they belonged to another lifetime.

I turned from the window and checked my phone. 6:50 PM. Ayush would be here any minute. My stomach twisted.

What had changed? I knew the answer. It was the internship—*that* damn internship.

I still remembered the day Ayush had shared the details with me, how excited I'd been, thinking this was our chance. But he'd won. And somewhere along the way, resentment had crept in, quietly, like a slow poison. And I'd let it grow.

I wiped my face and tried to refocus. Tonight wasn't about dredging up the past. It was just... a chance to reconnect. Or so I kept telling myself.

I wandered into the kitchen, checking the food for the third time in twenty minutes. Everything was still fine. The dal makhani was warm, the paneer curry looked perfect, and the naan was ready to heat. I'd gone all out, trying to recreate the kind of meals we used to enjoy together when things were simple.

Why did it feel like I was preparing for an exam?

My phone buzzed in my pocket, snapping me out of my thoughts. I pulled it out and glanced at the screen. It was a message from Ayush: *"Almost there. See you soon."*

A knot tightened in my chest. No backing out now. I replied quickly—*"Cool, see you soon"*—and slipped the phone back into my pocket.

Walking back into the living room, my eyes drifted to the bookshelf in the corner. On the top shelf, nestled between a couple of novels, was a framed photo. It was from that café in CP—the one Ayush and I used to frequent back in college. We'd taken the picture on one of our last visits before things started to shift. Both of us were grinning like idiots, arms slung around each other's shoulders, not a care in the world.

How had we gone from *that* to this awkward silence?

Just then, a knock. I froze, then shook off the nerves. It was just Ayush. Just my old friend.

Opening the door, there he stood—Ayush Malhotra. His face lit up with a smile, and for a second, it felt like nothing had changed.

"Hey, man," he said, stepping inside. "It's been a while."

"Yeah, it has," I replied, my voice slightly strained.

As Ayush walked in and shrugged off his jacket, I realized that this might not end as easily as I'd hoped. He still looked the same—confident, collected—but there was a flicker of uncertainty in his eyes.

We made small talk on the way to the dining table—work, mutual friends, pleasantries—but the air between us hung heavy with things unsaid.

As we sat to eat, I wondered if this dinner would start something new—or just remind us of what we'd lost.

"By the way, where's Aunty?" he asked, adjusting his chair.

"She's out of town—had to visit her village."

"I wish she was here. Never actually met her properly," he said.

"Maybe some other day," I replied, serving food onto the plates.

"Thanks for inviting me. I appreciate it."

You're appreciating it now. Let's see how you feel after a couple of hours.

"The pleasure's all mine," I said, passing him naan. I could feel it—tonight, we would finally break the ice.

"So, where did we leave off last time?" he asked, digging in. "Talking about careers at that café, right?"

Ayush picked up the conversation smoothly.

"We couldn't meet the last two Fridays," I said with a smile. "Could've been the same café but I had other plans."

"I know, right? How things change in an instant," he said, his eyes carrying a different weight.

I nodded. "Just like us..." he added.

The words hit me hard. Maybe he *did* want to talk about the distance. I froze but kept the conversation moving.

"Things change, people change. That's life."

"I agree. Anyway, what's happening lately? And by the way, this food is *delicious*," he said, licking his spoon. "I can't wait for your restaurant to open."

"Thanks, Ayush. I learned over the years. Don't cook often, but when I do, I enjoy it," I said. "Well, where do we begin?" I asked, hoping he wouldn't dive into the internship yet.

He thought for a moment. "Let's start with your career. How did you end up a writer when you had corporate dreams?"

His question sent me straight back to college.

"That's a good question," I said, zoning out briefly. "Well, you know, I opted for BMS, coming from commerce. I had a placement offer, so I went with it, figuring I'd see where it led."

"A lot of people do that. Skip forward."

"Right. In my second year at Hindu, I wasn't doing great. I explored various career options—professional courses, competitive exams, everything. But nothing clicked."

"You were bright. You could've cracked anything if you wanted to," he said.

"Thanks. Maybe. But I never saw myself in that race. I knew I was meant for something else."

"Writing books and opening a restaurant. Your purpose," he joked.

"I suppose. And then one day, I just knew."

"Knew what?"

"That I was going to become a writer. I'd always loved writing—not necessarily becoming famous—but I knew I'd be happy. I talked to my mother; she was sceptical at first but wanted me to be happy. From that moment, I started writing. My first book, right after second semester. It was tough, but I never stopped. I finished it before my fifth semester."

"That's inspirational. What's the title? I'm buying all your books!" he said, grinning.

"*Destiny*," I said, getting up to grab it from the shelf. I placed the book on the table.

"Wow! I'm so happy for you, Ramit. My friend wrote a whole novel and I didn't even know. I'm going to read all of your work."

"I hope you like them," I said, smiling. "Each book is a piece of me, crafted with love and passion."

"It shows. It shows in your eyes—you're full of pride. I'm proud of you," he said.

Time flew. We talked about everything, savouring the food. Before we knew it, three hours had passed. It was time for him to leave.

"Thank you, Ramit. For everything. You're an amazing chef too," he said, patting my shoulder. We laughed.

"Anyone can cook. But only the fearless can be great," I quoted.

"I see what you did there. Well, next time it's at my place. No excuses."

"Sure. I'll be there."

"You better be. I don't want things going down the shithole again."

As I looked into his eyes, I could tell—he was truly regretful for everything that had happened between us.

16
Chapter Sixteen

February 2024

The hectic examination phase at Delhi University had finally come to an end after nearly two to three months of late nights and early mornings. This time, it felt especially difficult, but I made it through. I believed I had given it a good shot. I expected to score a better grade that semester.

As the new academic year approached, I knew it wasn't going to be easy. I spent most of the vacation working and trying to improve my skills. I could have used the time more productively, but it was what it was. I wrote several poems and short stories —something I absolutely loved doing in my free time. Maybe I could become a great poet or an author someday.

It had been almost been a year since I first walked through the main gate of my college. It still felt surreal, as if time had flown by in the blink of an eye. I was no longer a junior, but a sophomore now. It felt great.

I had made some good friends in college, apart from the countless acquaintances. Samarth Katreja was one of my closest friends, even though we weren't in the same department. The same was true for Ayush Malhotra—he wasn't even in my college, yet we remained good friends. And then, of course, how could I forget her—Mayanti Sinha...

Undoubtedly, she was one of the best people I had met here, if not the best. I often wondered if things would have turned out this way had I not missed that metro that day. I believed that what's meant to be finds its way sooner or later. It had been a while since I last saw her, thanks to the exam season. But maybe that was for the best. I would have been far more distracted otherwise. I missed her. But I was sure we would meet again soon.

I needed to gear up for the sophomore year. People didn't really use the term around here, but I liked it — Sophomore. College was set to reopen in about eight or nine days, and I couldn't wait. Staying at home had become boring. I missed traveling to the North Campus. I missed attending boring lectures just because of the attendance rules. I missed my friends. I missed the hustle and bustle.

One day, while I lay on my bed doing nothing in particular, my phone beeped with a notification. It was a text message from Ayush.

Ayush: Hey! Wanna apply for an internship at MicroTech? I'm applying for it, so I thought of sharing it with you too. Fill out the form and they'll contact you accordingly.

Ramit: An internship at MicroTech?! You've got to be kidding me! Hell yeah, I'm up for it. Who would turn down such an opportunity? This could skyrocket our careers and portfolios. Thanks for this—I'll apply for it ASAP.

Ayush: No worries! All the best for this opportunity.

Ramit: We'll help each other with the preliminary tests and the interview. But you better watch out—I'm not going to hold back. Eyes on the target, or someone else will clinch it.

Ayush: Just wait and watch... we'll see who bags the internship.

Now I had something to focus on. The last few days had felt painfully slow. If only I had known about the internship earlier, I could have started preparing in advance. But better late than never.

I filled out the application form and began preparing for the preliminary test using online resources. It was a struggle finding good study material, but Ayush sent me some notes and guides. We helped each other through the preparation phase. The test was scheduled for the following month, and we did everything we could to secure a spot among the shortlisted candidates.

A week passed, and our colleges were about to reopen. I felt confident we could manage our preparation alongside classes, especially since it was the fest season in the Delhi University circuit. While other students would be busy enjoying events and parties, we would be working hard to grab the opportunity of a lifetime. Tough times bore fruitful results, and I was willing to make sacrifices. I was determined to work hard toward my goals with complete dedication.

The first day of the second year—or should I say sophomore year—finally arrived. I was looking forward to it. As I entered the campus, a wave of energy and excitement rushed through me.

ᏬᏬᏬ

Two Weeks Later,

College had reopened, and it felt good to be back—even though most of my attention was on the internship. There were four different preliminary tests that would shortlist the candidates for the final interviews. It was like a knockout tournament—fail one test, and you were out of the race. I had cleared two of them so far, and so had Ayush. As much as I was happy for him, I also knew he was going to be one of my strongest competitors in the selection round. It was shaping up to be a fierce competition.

Even though we had been preparing together through online sessions and by sharing study material, the underlying tension of rivalry remained. Ayush had been both supportive and competitive—and so had I. A little competition between friends never hurt.

Amidst all this chaos, I had started to pay more attention to my college studies as well. The first year had been a whirlwind. I knew that if I built a strong foundation now, it would be easier to get through the semester-end exams, regardless of the obstacles that came my way.

Life felt good when I was in love. It sounded like a cliché, but it was actually true. I had met Mayanti a few days ago after the college reopened. She seemed a bit different—maybe quieter than usual—or perhaps it just felt that way because I hadn't seen her in over sixty or seventy days. I hoped everything was fine with her.

Samarth on the other hand, who was busy preparing for his Chartered Accountancy Intermediate exams, which were scheduled for July. He was very serious about it. He told me he wouldn't be coming to college often this semester because he needed to focus entirely on his CA preparation. That meant one of my closest friends wouldn't be around much. It was unfortunate, but I hoped he achieved his goal. He truly deserved it.

The juniors hadn't arrived yet, the entrance exam results were still pending. Meanwhile, the college clubs and societies were gearing up for the welcome events and fresher's season. This was always one of the most fun times on campus.

I hoped this would be a great semester.

17
Chapter Seventeen

March 2024

"I'm going to do it," I said.

"Are you sure about that? Isn't it a bit too early?" Samarth asked, raising an eyebrow.

"I know this might sound sudden, but I've thought about it. She's the one, I'm destined to be with," I said. Samarth looked completely fazed—confused and uncertain.

"You see, love is glorious, but are you sure this is the right time to be in a relationship? You're just getting started—this might be the most crucial part of your life. You haven't even figured out your career path properly, and you're making statements like you've already chosen her as your life-long partner," he said without pausing. I leaned back in my chair and thought for a while.

"I know, *yaar*. This might not be the best time for all this. But I can't help myself. I truly believe she's the one. I've waited for a girl like this all my life—even though it's only been nineteen years. I won't let go of her. I swear to God, I can totally imagine spending the rest of my life with her."

"I mean, she's a good person. But are you sure she feels the same way about you?" Sam asked, concern written all over his face.

"That we'll see. I'll only know after I confess. After all, I've got to speak up. We've been great friends since we met, and we share a really special bond."

Samarth remained quiet. I understood his concern, but I had to confess before it was too late. "I know all of this might look childish and unrealistic. But I've believed in love all my life, and this time it just feels right. She's the one—the one. I can't keep it to myself anymore. She needs to know how I feel."

Samarth sighed, rubbing the back of his neck. I could tell he was worried for me, but I didn't care. I glanced out the window, watching the sunlight spill across the street. In my mind, I saw her face—the way her eyes lit up when she talked about her favorite things, or the way her laugh made the world feel a little less heavy.

"I'm just nineteen, and yeah, I should probably be thinking about grades, internships, or building my résumé. But when I think about my future, Samarth, she's there. I can see it so clearly—her beside me, us figuring life out together. It's not just a crush. It's something... more. She's it for me."

Samarth didn't say anything, but his furrowed brow said enough. I took a deep breath and continued, needing him to understand.

"Look, I know the risks. I know I might get rejected, and it might hurt like hell. But I can't let that stop me. You don't meet someone like Mayanti every day. She's not just another girl, Samarth. She's *the* girl. And yeah, maybe I'll fall flat on my face, but I'd rather take that chance than live the rest of my life wondering what could've been."

Mayanti was like my anchor, even if she didn't know it yet. She made life seem a hell of a lot better than it actually was.

"So... when are you going to do it?" he asked, arms crossed against his chest.

"The next time I meet her, when there aren't too many familiar faces around."

ᕤᕤᕤ

A couple of days passed after that conversation with Samarth. That's when I finally saw her in college. She had just walked out of the administration office, holding a bunch of documents in her hands. There weren't many people around. I thought this was the perfect moment to tell her how I felt. My heart was thumping like a drum, but I gathered some courage and walked toward her. I caught her by surprise. She looked a bit different today, as if something wasn't quite right—but regardless, I started the conversation.

"Hello there."

"Oh... Hi Ramit. How are you?" she asked.

"I am doing fine—but could be better. What's up? Why are you carrying that stack of documents?"

She glanced at them and muttered a few words, avoiding eye contact. "Well, I um... I needed to verify some documents at the college office. You know how hectic these things get. I just wanted to get it over with."

Her tone wasn't convincing. Something was definitely off. I could sense it. But I couldn't delay this any longer. I had to speak up.

"I see. Well... can I talk to you about something?"

"Right now?" she asked, trying to stuff the papers into her bag.

"Yes," I replied.

"I... Mayanti, I've been thinking a lot about us," I said slowly, choosing each word carefully. "About our friendship. About... everything."

She didn't respond at first, just stared at me, her eyes wide and searching. The silence stretched between us—heavy and full of unspoken words.

"I don't know when it happened," I continued, my voice barely above a whisper, "but somewhere along the way, I started feeling something more. And I know it's complicated, and maybe I shouldn't be saying this, but I can't keep pretending everything's the same."

Her eyes softened, and for a moment, I saw something flicker across her face—something that looked like understanding.

"Ramit..." she began gently.

I held my breath, waiting for her response, unsure of what she would say. But in that moment, it didn't matter.

"I need to tell you something too." Her eyes told me that something was definitely wrong.

I waited, holding my breath, my heart racing. I had finally said it—poured my heart out in a way I never thought I could. Mayanti stood there, her expression unreadable. Her lips parted, but no words came.

Then she finally spoke, her voice trembling slightly. "Ramit, I... I don't know what to say."

"You don't have to say anything right now," I replied quickly, forcing a smile to hide the weight forming in my stomach.

"Ramit, there's something I've been trying to tell you," she said, her voice so quiet it nearly vanished with the faint breeze. "Something I've wanted to say for a while, but I didn't know how."

I frowned, leaning a little closer. "What is it?"

She hesitated again, looking everywhere but at me. Then she took a deep breath and finally met my gaze. What I saw in her eyes sent a chill down my spine—regret, apology, and something else I couldn't quite place.

"I'm leaving," she said, barely above a whisper. "In two weeks. I'm going to New York for my studies."

Her words hit me like a freight train, knocking the air out of my lungs. I blinked, thinking I had misheard her. "You're... leaving?"

"I got accepted into a program I've always dreamed of—a full scholarship, Ramit. It's everything I've worked for."

My mind reeled, struggling to process her words.

"I've been trying to tell you," she added softly, "but I didn't want to hurt you. I didn't know how to say it."

A bitter laugh escaped before I could stop it. "And you chose now to tell me? Right after I pour my heart out to you?"

Her eyes glistened, but she blinked rapidly, refusing to let the tears fall. "But this is my dream, Ramit. I can't let it go."

"And what about us?" I asked, my voice raw and barely audible.

She flinched at the question, as if the very word us was too much to bear. "I don't know," she admitted. And those three words shattered whatever hope I had left.

Silence stretched between us—heavy and suffocating.

"Good luck in New York," I said at last, my voice hollow.

Her lips trembled. "Ramit, please don't hate me."

"I could never hate you," I said, the truth spilling out even as I turned to walk away.

I didn't look back. I couldn't.

That was the last time we spoke. For months afterward, her absence left a void I couldn't fill. I deleted her number, avoided places that reminded me of her, and threw myself into anything that could distract me from the ache she left behind.

18

Chapter Eighteen

November 2031

"You were really left heartbroken," Ayush said in a low voice, resting his hand on mine. "Well, I want to know more, and we'll certainly get there, but I don't want to make you sad or think about your past now. Let's talk about something else, shall we?"

"Yes, surely," I replied. "Okay then, tell me about you and Shalini. How did you two meet?" I asked him.

"Well—"

"We met four years ago, when I was looking for a friend at IIM Ahmedabad. And then, I bumped into him," Shalini said, putting food on the dining table for us.

"You know, right, I was lost and miserable in those days. It was my third day at IIM Ahmedabad. I was trying to figure out a few things, walking through the luxuriant green and huge campus, when I accidentally bumped into her—and that's when it all started," Ayush continued, giving a kiss to Shalini's hand. Her eyes sparkled with fondness. I couldn't help but notice how deeply they cared for each other. It made me feel warm and envious all at once.

"You make it sound so poetic," Shalini teased, sitting down at the table with us. "The truth is, he was just looking for someone to help him find the library, and I happened to be the unfortunate soul standing nearby."

Ayush laughed as he poured some water into our glasses. "Don't listen to her. She was the first person who made me feel like I wasn't entirely alone in that overwhelming place."

"It seems like destiny," I said, smiling at them. "You two are perfect together."

The conversation flowed effortlessly after that. Ayush and Shalini shared stories about their time at IIM Ahmedabad—nights spent cramming for exams, sneaking out for chai at midnight, and supporting each other through the pressure cooker that was business school. Their bond was palpable, and it was impossible not to admire the partnership they had built.

"I found my crutches when I was unable to walk, in Shalini. She held me through tough times. I was fortunate enough to have a partner like her," Ayush said, as his eyes met Shalini's.

"Truly a match made in heaven?" I said. As I listened, I found myself reflecting on the paths people take to find love and connection. It reminded me of my own feelings from long ago—feelings that I'd buried deep but had never truly let go of. I looked down at my plate, pushing food around with my fork as the memories of Mayanti crept into my thoughts.

"You okay, Ramit?" Shalini's voice pulled me back to the present. Her gaze was warm but inquisitive.

"Yeah," I replied quickly, forcing a smile. "Just... lost in thought."

"But seeing you two like this... it's inspiring. It makes me think about what I want in life."

The mood grew a little quieter after that, though it wasn't uncomfortable. Ayush steered the conversation toward lighter topics—funny stories from college, random quirks he'd noticed in me back then, and even embarrassing moments that had us laughing so hard, tears streamed down our faces.

But underneath it all, I couldn't shake the feeling that there was something left unsaid—some shadow of the past still lingering between me and Ayush.

ꕥꕥꕥ

March 2024

"I don't really get it. How could they reject me at this stage, when I cleared all the preliminary tests with a decent grade? Our marks were almost identical, one way or another. You made it, and they rejected me," I told Ayush on the phone.

"Well, the competition was very high. They've shortlisted ten candidates for the interview stage. I think you could've made it if your scores were just a little higher in certain tests," he said.

"I deserved a shot at the interview. I really think I did."

"Hard luck, I guess. Don't worry, you gained a lot of experience and knowledge preparing for this internship. That's what really matters at the end of the day. Don't go hard on yourself. You'll do just fine," he told me in a comforting yet confident voice.

"If it is what it is, then I'll let it be. Now, you must get that internship. If I can't be the one, then you should be," I said, both jealous and proud of him at the same time.

"Don't worry. I'll get it, after all—" he paused right there, as if he wanted to say something, "—I am the best." He chuckled jokingly. It felt like he was hiding something from me, but I didn't pay much attention to it, considering Ayush's nature.

"Look who's talking. I'll take your leave now. Bye. Good luck."

"Thanks man, I appreciate it."

I had really wanted that internship. It could have skyrocketed my career at this age—a dream internship for all of us. But well, fate had other plans. Let's see if Ayush would bag that internship or not. I really hoped he would, because he had helped me throughout the preparations as well. He deserved it too.

I was thinking of starting something really productive that would add a lot of value to my life and career. What were the things that I'd always wanted to do or achieve? Be a great musician or singer? I sang horribly, and I wasn't that good of a musician. Learn morse code? I was too lazy for that, and why would I even need to learn it? Obviously, I wasn't going to get into any situation in which I'd use Morse code to communicate. Maybe later—never.

Write a book? Hmm. I could do that. I had always wanted to write a book. It was one of my dreams, and I could use this time to write one. I had the skills and caliber to do it, so why not?

Let's start right now, and maybe I'd be done with my book in a year or two. That would be really great if I managed to pull off something like that. Mumma and everyone would be so proud and happy. I wouldn't tell anyone about it until I felt like it. I'd work on it—quietly, slowly and gradually. And when I'd be done, I'd show it to the whole world.

The problem was that when I started working on something like this, I would do it for a few days and then leave it as it was. I lacked consistency and productivity. I guessed I'd better start first and then work on being consistent with everything. I had a few ideas at the back of my head, and I would narrow down the choices into a list. Finalize an option and start on it right away.

I could be a great poet—or a writer. Maybe even a novelist. Who knows? I might just become one in the future. Destiny... I wondered where it would lead me.

Destiny...

19

Chapter Nineteen

November 2031

"WE GOT THE LICENSE!" I screamed with joy as I read the email sent by the government. I quickly logged on to the government website to check the status there as well. It showed all the details and flashed registered at the top of the document. I was elated!

"Mumma! Come and have a look at this," I called out as she came quickly, pacing herself.

"What happened?! Is everything alright?" she asked, worriedly.

"Alright? It's great! Look, here..." I pointed at the computer screen. She leaned forward to read it, and her eyes lit up with joy. After glancing through the document, she looked at me and embraced me with pure joy.

"We got the license. That's a big feat, I believe. It's not easy to get one, right?"

"Absolutely. Most people face difficulties at this stage of opening a business—and we got it, without any hassles," I said.

"Touchwood," she said, touching the computer desk. "Now, what's next?" she asked with intrigue.

"Next, we start contacting builders and contractors to lay the cornerstone and get the building constructed. We need to start arranging a lot of funds now. It's time we turn this dream into a reality," I answered. "I should call and tell Sam about this." I picked up my phone to dial up his number.

"Sure, go ahead. I'll continue the work I was doing. Do you need anything?"

"No, thanks," I replied while Samarth's phone rang. He picked up after a few seconds.

Ramit: "Hello?"

Samarth: "Hi Ramit? What's up?"

Ramit: "I have good news to share."

Samarth: "We got the restaurant license?"

Ramit: "How the hell do you know?! I legit feel like you're spying on me."

Samarth's laugh echoed through the phone.

"Ramit, come on. I know you too well. You've been obsessing over that license for weeks now. The only thing that could make you this excited is that email. So, am I right?"

"You're insufferable," I said, grinning. "But yes, we got it! It's official. We're in business—literally."

"That's incredible!" he exclaimed. "I'm so proud of you, man. This is the beginning of something huge."

"Thanks, Sam. Honestly, I couldn't have done this without you. From brainstorming ideas to crunching numbers late into the night—you've been there every step of the way."

"Don't get all sentimental on me now," he teased. "But seriously, this is your vision, Ramit. I'm just happy to be part of the journey."

I leaned back in my chair, feeling a mix of excitement and nerves. "The real work starts now, though. We need to get the building designed, and—oh, don't even get me started on securing funds."

"One step at a time," Samarth said firmly. "We'll figure it out, just like we've done with everything else. Have you thought about pitching to investors yet?"

"Not seriously," I admitted. "I was thinking of pooling in personal savings and maybe taking a loan. Investors mean giving up control—and you know how I feel about that."

"True," he agreed. "But it's worth considering, especially if we want to hit the ground running. Anyway, let's celebrate first. You've earned it."

I smiled. "You're right. Let's meet for dinner tonight. My treat."

"Done," he said. "See you at 8?"

"8 it is."

After hanging up, I leaned forward on the desk, staring at the glowing screen. The official license document was still open, and the sight of it filled me with a sense of accomplishment I hadn't felt in years. It was a validation of every sleepless night, every doubt, and every ounce of effort that had gone into this dream.

"Mumma," I called out again as I got up and walked into the living room. She was busy folding some clothes, her face still glowing with pride.

"I'm meeting him tonight to celebrate."

"You should," she said warmly. "You've worked hard for this moment. But remember, this is just the beginning."

"I know," I said, nodding. "There's a lot more to do, but I'm ready for it." As I stood there, I realized how much her unwavering support had meant to me throughout this journey. Even when I doubted myself, she never did.

I arrived at our usual spot, a cozy little diner tucked away on a quiet street. The familiar scent of spices and freshly baked bread hit me as soon as I walked in. Samarth was already there, seated at a corner table, scrolling through his phone.

"Right on time," he said, looking up with a grin as I approached.

"I was just about to order."

"You know me," I replied, sliding into the seat across from him. "Punctual as ever."

"Yeah, yeah," he said, waving over the waiter. We ordered the usual and waited for the food as the waiter left us in a comfortable silence for a moment.

"So," he began, "how does it feel? Knowing that your dream is finally taking shape?"

I smiled, leaning back in my chair. "Surreal, honestly. It's like… I've been chasing this for so long that now, standing on the edge of it, I feel equal parts excited and terrified."

"That's good. I would have been worried if you weren't terrified. You know it's real when you are terrified."

"So," Samarth said, breaking my thoughts, "what's next on the agenda? Have you started thinking about the actual construction process yet?"

I nodded. "Yeah, that's the next big hurdle. I've shortlisted a few contractors, but there's still the issue of funding. I was thinking of pooling personal savings and maybe a small loan."

"I genuinely did not expect something like this from you," Samarth said with a frown. He leaned forward, setting down his glass. "See, that's a good start. But the problem with these loans and debts is that you can get trapped in this never-ending loop of repayment—with hefty interest too."

I could see the concern in his eyes. I leaned back in my chair.

"I agree it's going to be difficult this way. But I don't want any investors getting on board because that means we giving away a lot of equity and freedom. Giving away a part… a part of our business. I don't think that I'm ready for that yet," I hesitated.

"I get it," he said, nodding. "But hear me out. What if the right investor wasn't just about money? What if they could bring something to the table—experience, connections, or even just credibility?"

I raised an eyebrow. "Do you have someone in mind?"

"Not actually. Do you?" he asked.

"Not yet," I replied.

The food arrived then, breaking the tension. As we dug into the steaming plates of butter paneer masala and naan, the conversation drifted to lighter topics—our college days, mutual friends, and, inevitably, Mayanti.

"So," Samarth said casually, between bites. "How's your headspace these days? Are you still… you know, thinking about her?"

I paused, my fork hovering mid-air.

"Sometimes," I admitted. "It's hard not to. She was such a big part of my life, even if it was for a short time."

Samarth nodded, his expression understanding. "You'll figure it out, man. But for now, focus on this. You've got something amazing here."

I smiled, grateful for his unwavering support. "Thanks, Sam. For everything."

As the dinner wrapped up and we stepped out into the cool night air, I couldn't help but feel a renewed sense of purpose. The road ahead was daunting, but with Samarth by my side and a plan taking shape, I knew I could face whatever came next.

"Well, you know Ayush Malhotra?" I asked him.

He looked up, thinking about the name—probably ringing some bells in his head, "Ayush Malhotra, the guy from Hansraj?"

"Yes, that guy. I met him a few months ago once again. Unexpectedly, at a metro station," I told Sam.

"Wow! That's surreal. You haven't talked about him in a very long time. How are you two catching up?"

"We met a couple of times at my place, a couple of times at his. Maybe a few times at our usual spot. I think our bond is getting re-established."

"That's some good news. I'd like to catch up with you two sometime. Have you talked about the past? I mean, about when you two stopped talking?"

"Not yet, but I guess we will pretty soon. We're meeting next week again," I said.

"Well, you gotta talk about it someday. All the best, Ramit. I hope things get better between you two."

Somewhere deep down inside, I wished the same as well.

I hoped things get better.

20
Chapter Twenty

April 2024

It was jarring to think about it. I just couldn't stop thinking about her—she's gone. Just like that? No, it couldn't be. For the first time in eighteen or nineteen years, it felt like I had found the one. The one who understood me, who shared a great bond with me. For the first time, I had fallen in love. A love that felt so good, everything seemed easy and beautiful. A smile that had engraved itself on the walls of my brain. Her sweet voice, the way she tucked her fingers to fix her hair—everything had felt so right. Until a few days ago, when she told me about her dreams. New York. The Big Apple.

Love was glorious, but it didn't take much to turn everything upside down. I did everything to remove her from my life—deleted her number, the chats, the pictures, everything. But it wasn't helping at all. I still loved her. I'd always love her. It might have sounded childish and immature, but I knew I had truly believed she was the one I was destined to be with for the rest of my life. With her, college had felt familiar and beautiful. But ever since she was gone, my eyes kept searching for her on campus. There was a pricking pain in the air, ever since she'd left.

My phone rang, jolting me from my thoughts. It took me a moment to realize it was buzzing on my desk. It was Ayush. I picked it up.

"Hey man, how are you?" he asked from the other end.

I gathered some liveliness in my voice, trying to lift the weight of pain and melancholy I was feeling.

"I'm doing fine... could be better," I said.

"I've got good news. I got the internship!" he replied quickly.

"Wow! That's great! You deserved it!" I cheered him on—it genuinely made me feel good, to some extent. We had both worked hard for that opportunity. If I couldn't get it, at least he did. That made me happy.

"Well, I called to tell you about this and thank you as well. You and I helped each other throughout the recruitment phase. Without that, neither of us could have come this far."

His words touched my heart. He had helped me too, despite the fierce competition.

"Hey. It's nothing to be thankful for. We're great friends, and that's what real friends do. You helped me too. We were in it together, and I'm glad you made it. I'm really happy for you. Genuinely," I said.

Ayush paused for a second, as if he were thinking about something.

"I appreciate that. I hope our bond stays strong, even after college," he said with a lot of faith in his voice.

"I wish the same, Ayush. When does the internship begin?" I asked.

"Seventeenth of April," he answered.

"That's great. I wish you all the best. Do well. I've got some unfinished work right now, so I'll take your leave."

"Yes, I will. No worries. Take care. Bye."

"Bye. Ayush. Bye."

The conversation ended on that note. It eased my pain a little. Now Ayush had work to do. I should also start working on something too—my book, my novel. It would help lift me out of this misery, and I could achieve one of my dreams at the same time. I had an idea and planned to mold it into a proper story and book starting the next day. This wasn't the end. I had to survive the hardships, no matter what. It was the only way out.

ᗐᗐᗐ

A Few Days Later

I visited Hansraj for a networking event. These events weren't common in Delhi University colleges—only the well-known North Campus ones hosted them once in a while. I thought it would be helpful to attend. After all, everyone kept saying networking was one of the key ways to excel in the cutthroat corporate world. And I hadn't met Ayush in a while. He could help me network more efficiently.

Upon reaching the college, I called him and asked that where he was. He said he was in the seminar hall. I quickly made my way there with some help. There were many small groups of five or six people standing around, getting to know each other. I searched for Ayush for a couple of minutes, and that's when I spotted him from behind, talking to a bunch of people in a circle. As I walked closer, his words became more audible in the noisy hall.

"Honestly, it's all about who you know. My uncle's recommendation was a game-changer. After that, the interview was a breeze," he said.

His words shook me. His uncle? What was this? When did that happen? I stopped in my tracks. Ayush had never mentioned this during our countless late-night conversations about internships. I shook my head, trying to maintain a straight face.

I gently tapped his shoulder. "Hi Ayush, were you talking about the MicroTech internship?"

He turned around quickly. "Hi Ramit! How are you? It's been a while. Here, meet these guys from SRCC." He shifted the topic swiftly, almost like he was trying to dodge something.

"Hello, everyone. I'm Ramit Bansal, currently pursuing BMS from Hindu College. Ayush and I met on our first day of our university." I greeted everyone and shook hands as they introduced themselves. But I couldn't stop thinking about what Ayush had said.

"Well, I'll see you around. Can you excuse us for a minute?" Ayush said to the group. They nodded and dispersed.

"Hey Ramit, I hope it wasn't hard to find the seminar hall. How's everything?" he asked.

"It wasn't too hard. You tell me—how's the internship going?"

"It's great. It gets a little bit hectic, but I'm managing. It's a great opportunity."

I knew he was hiding something. I had to bring it up.

"That's great. By the way… what were you telling those guys when I arrived? Something about your uncle helping with the internship?" I asked.

He paused briefly. "Ayush?" I said again.

"Well, about that… I've been meaning to tell you for a while but never found the right moment. My uncle knew the HR head at MicroTech and helped me get an interview. But I still had to earn it," he admitted.

Wait—what? His words broke me. Ayush had help all along? That's how he got the interview? No, he would've told me… right?

"Ramit. It wasn't a big deal," he said.

Not a big deal? I wanted to laugh. While I had been stressing over the prelims, he had a foot in the door? And he let me believe we were equals?

"So while I was working so hard, you already had a foot in the door?" My voice was sharper than I intended.

Ayush frowned. "Come on, Ramit. You're making it sound like I didn't earn it. I worked hard too."

"Yeah, sure," I muttered, bitterness slipping out.

The room seemed to fall silent. "Do you even realize how much I trusted you? I thought we were supposed to be each other's driving force."

"Come on, man. You're making it sound like I didn't earn it. I worked hard too," he said.

"Yeah. Sure," I muttered, bitterness curling in my chest.

He opened his mouth, but I didn't let him speak.

"But while I was giving it my all, you knew everything and never told me. You could have at least been honest. It wasn't that hard, was it?"

"I wanted to… but never found the right moment, Ramit—"

I cut him off. "You know what? All those things they say about college friendships? They were right. When did I realize that? Right now. This stupid goddamn moment."

"Were you afraid I'd find out that you didn't *actually* earn it?"

The words had barely left my mouth when it happened.

Crack.

Ayush's hand struck my cheek with a sharp, echoing slap.

For a second, everything around us fell into silence — even the murmurs from nearby circles froze mid-air.

My face stung, but not as much as the shock.

He stood still, breathing hard, his eyes burning — not with anger, but betrayal. "Don't you dare say I didn't earn it," he said, his voice shaking. "You think you're the only one who struggled? The only one who had dreams? I worked hard too, Ramit. I just didn't think I had to justify every step of my journey to you."

People around us had begun to glance in our direction, sensing the tension. But neither of us cared.

I stared at him, speechless. I wanted to yell. I wanted to cry. But more than anything, I wanted to rewind everything and stop this from happening.

Instead, I turned around and walked out, each footstep louder than the last. The space between us had grown heavier — thick with things left unsaid. I had always believed in Ayush, in our friendship. But in that moment, that belief felt like a joke.

ᐅᐅᐅ

The silence echoed again, even now. It felt like the clock had turned back to April 2024, to that same seminar hall. Shalini looked at us both. Then Ayush finally broke the silence.

"You never tried to contact me, Ramit? Why?" His voice was deeper now. "That was the last time I saw you or spoke to you. You just left the hall, you didn't pick up my calls, didn't reply to my texts. And then... you blocked me."

"Ayush, I'm sorry," I said quietly.

"You're sorry? Do you even realize how difficult it was for me too?" he said.

I struggled to find the right words. I took a deep breath, gathering my thoughts.

"Ayush, I really am sorry. I know what I did was immature. I was immature back then. Maybe I still am sometimes. But that's human, right? I made mistakes. I was deeply hurt. I felt betrayed that day—because you used your connections to get that internship. That stupid MicroTech internship. You slapped me in a crowded seminar hall. That was wrong, Ayush."

He stood up and walked toward me, resting his hand on my shoulder.

"I should've told you. I didn't plan on hiding it... I just didn't want you to think I had an unfair advantage."

"But you had one," I shot back without thinking.

"Yes, I did. But I know I let you down. That's what I was afraid of. I had to crack that interview on my own—no help, no strings. And I did. But still, I get it. I understand why you felt that way."

He paused. "But think about it, Ramit—it was just an internship. At the time, it felt like everything. We were young and passionate. But it shouldn't have been the reason for our fallout. We were great friends, and we let that internship get between us."

I looked into his eyes and saw regret written all over his face.

My mind felt like a mess of emotions — regret, anger, shame. I wanted to speak, to apologize again, but Ayush started talking first.

"You weren't just my friend — I trusted you. And when you walked away... it felt like I lost someone important."

"I know," I muttered, my chest tightening. "I know I overreacted... but it didn't feel like just an internship. It felt like proof that I wasn't good enough. Like everything we worked for meant nothing. That slap felt like an insult. Do you even realize, how I felt when you did that?"

Ayush stood up from his chair. His face was a mix of exhaustion and hope — like he wasn't sure if we could fix this or if I even wanted to try. He took a step forward.

"I'm sorry," he said. "For everything."

His shoulders slackened, like he'd finally let out a breath he'd been holding for years. Then, we hugged — years of silence dissolving in a moment.

As I held him, I realized something—maybe this wasn't about the internship at all. Maybe I was just scared. Scared that Ayush had outgrown me, and I couldn't keep up. But now, none of that mattered.

For the first time in years, I felt like I had my friend back.

21
Chapter Twenty-One

May 2024

"And with that, we're going to end today's lecture. I hope you all have a good day ahead," Professor Anand said, dismissing the class. The students filed out one by one, leaving just the two of us behind. We both began packing our bags to leave.

As I was putting my stationary and other items into the bag, I suddenly noticed someone standing near me.

"Hi Ramit, is everything okay?" he asked.

Was his sixth sense working? Did he already know I wasn't doing well? Was it that obvious I was feeling melancholic?

Still, I tried to put on a brave face. "Yes sir, I'm doing fine," I replied. I paused for a second. "I guess…"

"I guess?" He looked at me, slightly concerned. "Something seems off. You know you can talk to me about anything—if I can help, I will."

His words touched me.

"Thank you so much, sir. Can I talk to you about it now?" I asked, a faint glimmer of hope in my voice.

"Yeah, sure. I don't have any more lectures today," he said.

"Sir, I don't know how to put it into words. I feel lost these days. I'm going through a really tough phase. It feels like God is putting me through some incredibly difficult test. A lot has happened lately, and it all happened so fast. I'm not able to keep up with any of it." I looked out of the the window to my left.

"I fell in love with someone, and she left the country to pursue her dreams. All the way to New York. I made a good friend at another college... that didn't end well either. I felt betrayed. I lost an internship opportunity that could've been career-changing. I've started doubting myself. I feel like a loser. Like someone destined to lose in this game of life."

"That's the problem, I see..." He studied me for a moment. "Let me try and break this down for you, okay?"
I nodded.
"First of all, you said you lost an internship. Right?"

"Right. An internship at MicroTech," I said.
"MicroTech? Wow, that would've been a great opportunity. But let's try looking at it differently. You must've prepared for the preliminary rounds, the tests, the interviews. You went through all of that, right?"
"Yes sir, I did."
"I get it. The goal was to get the internship. But even if that didn't happen, you gained a lot in the process—knowledge, experience, maybe even some clarity. That will help you later. Who knows? You might get an even better internship. Or maybe a full-time job offer down the line."
He smiled gently.
"Now, about your friend. I understand you felt betrayed. I won't ask for details. All I'll say is, it's always your decision—whether to cut ties or try again. You can always go back and attempt to rekindle something, but that choice is yours. If you think they're not worth another try, then don't overthink it."

I listened closely. I'd always disliked people who handed out 'divine insights' like fortune cookies, but Professor Anand was different. He wasn't preaching. He was just being honest—and insightful.

"I hope you're getting my point."

"Yes sir, I am. Totally," I replied.

"People come into your life and stay for a while. Some leave after playing their part. Maybe they'll return someday, maybe they won't. But one thing's for sure—you have to keep the cycle of life moving. No matter how low you feel, you have to keep going."

"That's true," I said, nodding in agreement.

"As for the love part…" He paused. "I won't say much. I'm probably not the best person to give advice on that. But it's good to be hopeful. Just be prepared for the worst-case scenario too."

His expression shifted—hopeful to heavy, in an instant. I wondered what memory flickered through his mind when he said that.

"I'll try my best," I said. "It must be getting late for you, sir. We should get going."

"Sure. I just hope my words help. Don't stress over things too much. You never know who might walk into your life the very next minute. People come and go—but you've got to keep moving, with a handful of hope."

As he finished, a knock came at the door.

We both turned.

Standing there was a not-so-familiar face.

"Good afternoon, sir. Are you Professor Anand?" she asked.

"Yes, I'm Anand. Come in," he said.

"Hello Sir, I'm Tamannah Sharma. I just migrated from Miranda House," she said, extending her hand. Bold move, I thought.

Anand shook her hand. "Welcome to Hindu. I hope you'll have a great time here."

I stood there awkwardly beside them, unsure whether I should stay or leave.

Then suddenly—

"Hello there! Your good name?" she said to me, catching me off guard.

I collected myself and shook her hand. "Hi! I'm Ramit. Ramit Bansal."

"And I'm Bond. James Bond," she said, in a perfect Sean Connery accent, laughing. Even Anand Sir couldn't help but grin. I looked at her, then at him—and found myself chuckling too.

"Just kidding! Please don't mind," she said. Then she turned back to the professor. "It was a struggle finding you, sir. I checked the staff room, then your colleagues pointed me to your timetable. It was hard finding this room, but I finally made it. I wanted to ask if I could still enrol in your course. Even if it's from the beginning, I'm willing to start now. Is that possible?"

"Yes, you can join. But there's a catch—you'll have to complete it even after graduation. If that's okay with you, then you're welcome to attend from next week. We haven't covered much yet."

"Oh, that's not a problem. But tell me—do you really think it's worth pursuing after graduation? Be honest."

"I might be biased," he said, smiling. "But I'd recommend it to anyone even remotely interested in the field. You can ask him too," he added, gesturing toward me. She turned and looked me straight in the eyes.

"Well... I've always been interested in psychology and things like this. That's why I chose it. Also, one of the biggest reasons was Anand sir himself. I met him briefly before I picked this subject. Do you remember that day, sir?"

"Oh yes, I certainly do. You met me in my resource room. I remember it clearly. *Ek woh din tha,* when someone came to me personally to ask about the subject, *aur ek aaj ka din hai,*" he said, glancing at both of us.

"It was honestly one of the best decisions I've made. He is a great teacher—and more importantly, a wonderful human being," I said. Anand sir chuckled and patted my back.

"We were having quite an insightful conversation before you came," I said. "He's one of the finest I've ever come across my entire life."

Anand sir started walking toward the door slowly, almost shy under the praise.

"I think you two will get along well," he said. "Why don't you two chat a bit while I head out? Take care, Ramit. Hope to see you in class, Tamannah. Have a good day."

With a big smile, he exited the room.

I picked my bag up and looked at Tamannah, who stood by the desk adjusting the strap of her tote bag. There was a quiet confidence in her—not loud, just... steady.

"So... Ramit," she said, tilting her head slightly, "what do you guys usually talk about in these lectures? Is it always this intense?"

I laughed lightly, brushing away the heaviness of the last half-hour. "Not always. Sometimes we talk about case studies. And sometimes... we just talk about life."

"I've always loved doing that. Talking about life—and everything in between. Also, I've always been fascinated by how people work. What drives them. What breaks them."

"You talk like you've seen some things," I replied, curious now.

She smirked. "Haven't we all?"

"So," she said again, "where's the best chai on this campus? If I'm going to be stuck here for another year, I might as well start with the essentials."

I chuckled. "You're in luck. There's this stall near the behind the canteen. *Uncle ke haath ki chai* — elite level."

"Lead the way then, Mr. Bansal," she said, slinging her bag onto her shoulder.

And just like that, the weight of the day felt a little lighter.

We had just been talking—Anand sir and I—about people entering your life and playing a small, meaningful role. And then, just like that, Tamannah entered mine.

I didn't know if she was going to be a passing chapter or something more permanent. But for now, I was simply grateful she showed up—with her Bond jokes, her warmth, and her perfectly timed arrival.

22
Chapter Twenty-Two

May 2024

It had been a few days since that conversation with Professor Anand, but his words hadn't left me—not even for a second.

"People come into your life and stay for a while. Some leave after playing their part. Maybe they'll return someday, maybe they won't."

I found myself replaying that line again and again. What defines that 'part'? How do you know when someone's chapter in your life is over—and what if you misread the whole thing?

He had said it so simply, as if it were just another lecture, another passing line—but it stayed with me. I began myself looking at people more carefully. Noticing the fleeting nature of their presence. Watching how strangers brushed shoulders in the Metro, how friends drifted apart without ceremony. I thought of Mayanti, of Ayush, of how easily people could disappear from your life without a real goodbye. Some of them were forced to drift apart, and with some, it just happened. You're never really sure of what's next. Is it over? Is their 'part' done in your life?

That stupid goddamn question was going to linger around my head for a while.

And then, without intending to, I thought of her—Tamannah Sharma.

We'd only met once. A chance encounter, really. But there was something about her—something disarming in her energy, and that strange mix of warmth and wit. I remembered her voice, that playful *"Bond. James Bond."* It still made me smile.

I hadn't seen her since that afternoon. All I knew was that she might not take that course—maybe she had changed her mind. Some part of me was curious to know how she looked at this small world. She seemed to carry a kind of confidence, which was... steady. Not dominating.

A Few Days Later – The Classroom

It was a Thursday. Not many folks were around on campus, probably because the weekend was approaching and not much time had passed since the semester began. Most students were spending time with their families in their hometowns. Professor Anand hadn't arrived yet, but a few students had already taken their seats, heads bowed over notebooks and early—morning yawns. Just as I settled on one of the seats, I heard the door open.

She stepped in quietly—Tamannah. She had actually come.

She noticed me almost instantly. There was that same spark in her eyes. The one that told you she wasn't just observing the world—she was *reading* it. Through the lens of her eye, someone who looked at everything as if it meant something significant.

"Hey! Fancy seeing you again," she said, walking over.

"I wasn't sure if you'd actually join the course," I replied.

"Neither was I," she shrugged. "But after that whole staff room scavenger hunt and your glowing review, I figured it was worth a try."

I chuckled, remembering that chaotic introduction. She slid into the seat next to me.

Professor Anand entered a minute later, smiling his usual composed smile. He greeted the class, scanned the room briefly, and gave a small nod when his eyes landed on her.

"Good to see you again, Ms. Sharma. I'm glad that you chose this subject. Welcome."

She offered a polite smile.

"Today," Anand began, "since there are not many students present, we'll be talking about something I hold close to my heart. It's not a scientific theory in the traditional sense, but rather a poetic one. A metaphor. I was thinking about it the other day, when I was returning home, driving down the road. Some call it the 'Invisible String Theory.' Has anyone heard of it?"

"A string," he continued, "an invisible thread that connects us to certain people. Across time, across distance. Sometimes we meet them early, sometimes much later. But they're tied to us in ways we can't explain. Maybe they always were."

The lecture went on. But I wasn't really focused anymore.

My mind kept wandering. To threads. To connections. To people who enter our lives and stay just long enough to change something—without ever realizing it.

That particular thought, that theory, that string... All of it kept me fascinated.

The lecture ended, and Anand left us with a theory that was both meaningful and impactful.

"Have you ever felt that 'string' tied to you?"

A soft voice pulled me out of my thoughts.

Tamannah looked at me and asked, "Have you?"

"I have. Do you?" I countered.

"Every single day. I had read about this theory briefly before. But today's lecture gave me a more detailed and vivid vision. I can't stop thinking about it now. Such a beautiful theory, isn't it?" she said, turning her head toward me.

I nodded with a smile on my face. She looked up once, hesitated, then smiled lightly.

"Want to walk for a bit?" she asked, slinging her tote bag over her shoulder.

"Feels wrong to go straight home after a lecture like that."

"Yeah, sure. I was thinking the same. I like to wander around—with my thoughts and feelings. Especially after something like this. Come on. Let's go."

I got up from my seat and stood by the classroom door, waiting as she gathered her things in an unhurried manner.

We walked side by side through the shaded parts of the campus building. Leaves rustled by, and the wind filled the air with a serene stillness.

"You looked like you were really into what he said," Tamannah said after a while.

"Yeah," I nodded, half-smiling. "It's just... funny how some things stay in your mind even after the person who said them has walked out the door. He's one of those people."

"Hmm." She tucked a strand of hair behind her ear. "Strings. Connections. I like the idea of it."

"Even if they're invisible?" I asked.

"Especially if they're invisible," she said. "I think the strongest ones always are."

A small silence followed. And again—it wasn't uncomfortable.

If anything, it felt like something was gently being built between us.

The kind of friendship that doesn't need loud declarations to be real.

The kind of bond that doesn't really require much effort. The one that just happens on its own, so effortlessly.

We spent the next few minutes introducing ourselves and talking to each other about our lives and interests. She was from English Honours, with a soft corner for books and a habit of scribbling thoughts she didn't always show the world. She had left Miranda not because she hated it, but because she wanted to be part of something different. Something that felt like a part of her own story—just like they showed it in the movies.

She wanted 'Hindu' to be the backdrop of her own film—where she was the main character and the world revolved around her.

We exchanged our contact numbers and social media profiles—just to stay in touch.

Who knows, maybe this was the beginning of something special for both of us.

It already felt that way. Ever since the moment she had walked into the classroom that day, something had shifted. As if the invisible string had been tugged, drawing us closer.

I believed it. And I hoped she felt it too.

We ended up near the campus café, not quite realizing how far we'd walked.

I bought us both a cup of tea, and we sat under an old tree with a worn-out bench beneath it. Sunlight filtered through the leaves like it was trying to listen in on our conversation.

"I didn't expect to meet someone like you here," Tamannah said, out of the blue.

I looked at her. "Someone like me?"

"You know... someone who's thinking just as much. Who writes. Who listens."

She sipped her drink. "People don't always listen."

I chuckled, lowering my eyes. "I'll take that as a compliment. A good listener. Yeah, well... I've been learning how to."

We both smiled, and our eyes met for a brief second.

Like two people noticing that maybe, just maybe, the invisible thread was already tugging.

Not with love, not yet—

But with something else.

Something real.

23

Chapter Twenty-Three

July 2024

The sky was a soft blur of grey and peach. Tamannah and I had found a quiet spot near the college canteen and sat there with our cups of coffee. Neither of us liked the coffee much, to be honest, but we didn't want to get up either.

"I like this weather," Tamannah said, tucking a loose strand of hair behind her ear. "It's like it wants to pour down, but doesn't want to, at the same time."

I smiled faintly, looking toward the sky, my eyes fixed on the horizon. "Yeah. It holds everything in... until it can't."

Tamannah glanced at me, letting the silence grow a little —easy and unforced.

Then, I said it. "My mother's name is Anubhuti."

She turned her head to face me, surprised by the sudden shift in topic.

"She... went through a lot when I was a kid. My father was never like a father. He was the kind of weather you couldn't prepare for — sharp, sudden, and always destructive. Just like a hurricane, spinning through our lives again and again... and again."

She listened quietly, giving me her full attention.

"All those years, both of us faced a lot of misery. There were days when he even tried to kill us. I still remember some instances vividly. He once tried to take my mother's life by strangling her—"

"Oh dear Lord! I'm so sorry for what happened to you and her," she interrupted, shocked.

"There's something I wrote once," I said, eyes fixed on the chipped edge of the bench we sat on.

"A poem?" Tamannah tilted her head.

I nodded. "Yeah. From a long time ago. But I still remember every word."

Then, with the evening light falling over us, I recited:

Long Ago...
Not so very long ago...
We both were going through a lot of agony...
Helpless and miserable...
Those nights...
Still send shivers down my spine
Oh good Lord!
Don't ever make someone go through misery like we did...

I still remember that night,
When he tried to end it all in one stroke...
An attempt to strangulate and choke...
I witnessed it all with my teary eyes...

I tried to scare him off with my plush lion cub.
It didn't work, I thought it was all over...
I turned my face toward the wall, terrified and petrified...
Felt feeble and weak, started to weep silently...

One glance was all it took, you looked at me...
Gouged his eyes, kicked him and struggled...
Fought back like a warrior...
Took me and ran away...

In those melancholic times,
You did everything you could to see me grin and smile...
You were in extreme pain but made sure that I would never be afflicted...
You held on to me when I needed it...

All I can do is assure you,
You will never ever be forlorn
I will never let go and hold on
I will always have your back and hold on... Hold on... Never let go...

When I finished, Tamannah didn't speak. Not immediately. She just looked at me — really looked.
As if every silence between the lines had found a home in her eyes.

"That wasn't just a poem, Ramit," she said softly. "It felt like... a memory someone had locked away in their chest for years. The kind that hurts and heals at the same time. You write like you're not trying to impress anyone. Just... telling the truth. That's rare."

I thanked her for the compliment and continued.

"Imagine your father holding you off the fifth-floor balcony, about to drop you. Those days were really tough." I sighed. "Well, it was pretty unfortunate, but things couldn't go on like that forever. One day, my Mumma decided to leave that hell. She faced a lot, but in the end, the one with resilience and courage won the battle. I don't think I'd be alive, talking to you right now, if my Mumma hadn't fought back. We fought the divorce case for five years — and we won."

"YAY! That's great," she said in a gleeful voice.

"She lived for me. If she hadn't fought back that night, I wouldn't be here talking to you today. I know that for sure. Now it's my turn to give her everything she wants."

A soft breeze passed. Tamannah's hand, still holding her cup, rested just a little closer to mine.

"I think that's when I learned to stay quiet. To stay hidden. But Ma... she never really could. She held me together, even when no one was holding her."

"You know what? You are God's child. I'm so happy for you and Aunty. That you two came out of that shitty situation. I really hope no one has to go through what you went through. It must have been so difficult," she said, and rested her hand on mine gently.

"Thank you. I don't talk about this much. Thank you for being a patient listener," I said.

"No worries. I got to know more about you. Also, I would love to meet Aunty someday," she said excitedly.

"Yeah, sure! She'd love meeting you too. We'll make it happen one day or another," I promised.

The campus was filled with students that day. As the silence settled between Tamannah and me, I saw a familiar figure in the distance — slightly hunched, hands in his pockets. Wandering aimlessly. Samarth.

There was something off about his walk. It lacked its usual rhythm. I took out my phone and dialed his number.

"Where are you going?" I asked gently once the call connected.

Samarth sounded surprised. "Nowhere. Just walking."

"Come to the usual spot, *yaar*. I'm here... and someone's with me."

There was a pause. Then a quiet, "Okay."

Tamannah tilted her head. "Friend?"

"Yeah," I nodded, pocketing the phone. "One of the best I've had."

She scooted aside, making room on the bench as if she already knew someone needed it. A few minutes later, Samarth arrived. His face wore that same carefully crafted half-smile — polite but empty. His eyes were tired, maybe more than tired.

I stood up and pulled him into a brief side hug. "Tamannah, meet Samarth. Samarth — Tamannah."

Tamannah smiled warmly, a small nod accompanying her greeting. "Hey. I've heard a little about you."

Samarth returned the smile, but his gaze was already slipping away, lost in some thoughts and calculations running quietly in the back of his mind.

He didn't sit immediately.

"You alright?" I asked.

"Yeah," he said automatically. Then, after a beat, "Just... exam season. You know how it is."

Tamannah softly asked, "What exams?"

"CA Inter," both of us said in unison.

"Must be tough," Tamannah said.

He didn't reply for a few seconds. Then he sank onto the bench, sighing into his hands. "It's not the exam, honestly. It's... me."

Tamannah stayed quiet, giving him space. I placed a hand on his shoulder. "You've always worked hard. You'll be fine."

Samarth looked at me. "I don't know, Ramit. This time, it feels like I'm carrying something I don't know how to drop."

I took out the water bottle out from my bag and handed it to him. "Here. First of all, drink some water. You look pretty distressed."

He took it and drank a few sips from the silverware bottle I always carried.

"Listen to me now. I know it's tough to manage all the stress and pressure during exam season. But the key to acing exams is using that stress in a beneficial way. It's also known as—"

"Eustress," Tamannah completed my sentence and smiled at me. We learned about it in Anand's class.

"Exactly. You're experiencing distress, which isn't helpful at all. Just have faith in yourself. Give it your best shot, and the rest will follow. What matters is how you face your battles and the approach you take — to put up a brave front and even convert failure into success."

I didn't know if this pep talk would help, but I knew one thing for sure — I could be a guiding light for people, even if I wasn't doing well myself.

Samarth stood up and turned to me. "You're right, Ramit. But a lot of people — relatives, especially — will criticize me. I skipped most of my college classes to study for Inter. That's made my CGPA hit the rock bottom. What am I left with? A not-so-good CA preparation. *Na college theek se ho paa raha, na CA Inter. Samjh hi nahi aa raha kya karu?"*

"*Aree. Thoda Rest Kar.* I know it's important for your career but don't overthink *itna zyada.* Wanna go out and eat something?My treat.It'll take some load off your head. Tamannah will join us, right?" I turned to her, and she nodded with a faint smile.

"I appreciate it, Ramit. But not today. I still have a lot to revise. I should devote my time to studies right now. Maybe it's best. You guys have fun. I'll take your leave," he said, giving me a hug and Tamannah a gentle handshake before leaving.

I sat on the bench again and watched him walk away from the campus crowd —eyes on the ground, head dejected. His shoulders carried a weight that wasn't his. He seemed off these days.

"Your friend seems very tired. Is he okay?" Tamannah asked, as we both watched Samarth leave.

"I don't know. He's one of the most hardworking students I've ever met. It must be something serious if he's feeling this burden. I'm worried for him," I said. "Shall we walk? To the Metro Station?"

"Yeah, we should. It's getting late. I need to study for the tests as well," she replied.

As we started walking, she said something that really got me into thinking. "People around us — *jinke saath hum time spend karte hai,* we share our joys and sorrows, laugh out loud with each other... But deep down, we never really know what's going on inside someone's mind. Behind every smile, there could be a pain. A silent cry for help."

Those words moved me. It was a sad truth — and a reality of today's world.

"You're absolutely right. Sometimes, even the ones who sit the closest feel like they're a thousand miles away. And the truth is — pain doesn't always knock loudly. It's like a silent disease, hollowing you out from within. Until one day, when it becomes too evident to ignore."

"The problem is that the people we think are close to us don't always share their sorrows. They hide it. We don't open up easily. Am I making sense?" she asked.

"Yes, absolutely. There's a trust issue. It takes time to build a bond where we're not judged, and where constant support is offered, unconditionally. That's the harsh reality."

Tamannah nodded. "I've met people who carry so much pain and yet pretend like everything's fine. And the scary part is, they get so good at pretending... they forget how to stop."

I didn't say anything for a few seconds. "I used to be one of them. Maybe I still am."

She looked at me, a gentle honesty in her eyes that made the air feel warmer. "You opened up today. That's rare. And brave."

"It's easier with you," I told her.

"There's a dire need for friends and people who can really listen to you. People can't go on alone. You need support at the end of the day. A cornerstone."

I looked at her, amazed by the way she delivered those words so poetically. No wonder why she opted for English Hons. "That was... metaphorical," I complimented her.

She chuckled. "Will you be my cornerstone?"

"Cornerstone?" I asked.

"You know... the first stone laid at the foundation of a building. The one everything else rests on. I don't mean forever or in every way... but maybe just for now. Just while you and I figure things out."

I didn't reply right away. There was a stillness between us again — not from hesitation, but from the weight of something meaningful settling in.

"Then let's build," I finally said. "One stone at a time."

24

Chapter Twenty-Four

The Next Morning – July 2024

I woke up earlier than usual. Not from a dream—but with the lightness that usually follows after letting out something that had been trapped deep within inside for too long. The room was quiet. I stared at the ceiling fan spinning slowly above my head, thinking about the day before — Tamannah's voice, the way she had listened to me without interrupting, and that one word which echoed and stayed with me even now:

Cornerstone.

I sat up on the edge of the bed and let the moment linger. There was this new energy I could sense rising inside me. It felt like the cracks in me weren't flaws, but small spaces through which light could enter. My spirit was healing. I reached for my journal, which I had stopped writing in a few weeks ago, when life had begun to feel like either too much or nothing at all. This morning, the words came easily, and I started writing once again.

July 21, 2024 — 7:14 AM

<u>*Healing, slowly but surely…*</u>

It's been a while since I last journaled. Life has been nothing short of a roller coaster. It's gone up and down—mostly down, though. May was such a low point in my life. I had never felt so lost in my entire life ever before. Mayanti, the girl who I loved with all my heart, just left—so unexpectedly. I lost a friendship too and I still don't know whether it was a good decision to cut off ties with him, after all the moments we had shared.

My psychology teacher, Anand Krishnan, became a guiding light during those dark days. He was more than just a professor—like a friend, a companion. He's one of the best teachers I've ever had in my 19-20 years of my life. He helped me get through those problems, at least to some extent. His words of wisdom were always thought-provoking. And then, one day, while I was talking to him about how people enter and exit from our lives once their part is done, someone entered mine.

Tamannah Sharma. She's changed the way I look at life. She didn't do anything extraordinary—maybe it was just the way she listened to me. Completely. Without judgement. There's something different about her. Her presence just makes everything feel so easier. She reminds me of still mornings after a storm—not loud or dramatic, but quietly reassuring. There's a kind of tranquility in the air when she's around.

Tamannah never pried into my past. Not until I felt ready. And even when I told her everything—about Ma, about the childhood we survived, about the silence that wrapped around our home like a noose—she didn't give me pity. She gave me presence. A soft kind of understanding no one had offered before.

She looked at me after I'd shared it all, and said,

"I think you're braver than you know. Carrying all that pain and still choosing to be kind—that's not weakness, Ramit."

And for the first time in months, I believed that maybe—just maybe—I wasn't broken. That I could be soft and still survive.

I don't know what the future holds—for her, or for me. I just know that, in this moment—we're holding space for each other.

And that... that feels like enough.

ݕݕݕ

I closed the journal and got up from my desk. I walked to the balcony, where I saw the sunrise spreading its rays across the horizon. I felt each and every golden beam on my skin, as if they were healing me. Fixing all those scars and cracks that had left me lifeless. I wanted to live. I wanted to play this game of life, regardless of what the future held. I wanted to cherish each and every moment—and go with the flow.

"Got up so early?"

I turned and looked behind me to find Mumma, holding a newspaper in her hand.

"Good morning, Mumma."

"Good morning, *bachcha*," she said, sitting in one of the balcony chairs.

"Yeah, I got up early. Just one of those days," I said, dragging the other chair into place.

"What days?" she asked, looking out toward the skyline.

"Days when you feel like holding on to hope. When you need it the most," I said, pointing toward the beautiful sunrise.

"Isn't that beautiful? Isn't that worth living for? I love the Sun when it shines. I love it," I said, looking at Mumma, who was smiling from ear to ear as she listened.

"You're right. It is. I wonder what went through your head when you woke up this morning," she chuckled, unfolding her newspaper.

"Good people, good thoughts, and hopeful new beginnings."

"Well, then, how's everything lately? I assume it's going great," she said, glancing at the articles.

"I wouldn't say everything is great—and that's completely fine. It doesn't need to be. Nothing is perfect, and it never will be. But yes, I'm trying to fight my battles with all my might, and hopefully, the Sun will rise on me once again."

"You're truly up to something. Tell me—what's changed your outlook so quickly," she said, tilting her gaze upward.

"Nothing much. I met a couple of good souls who've been really supportive lately. One of my professors and a new friend—Tamannah. Both of them have cemented their places in my life in such a short time that I can't even imagine how dull my life would've looked without them."

"Aree waah… I'm glad to hear this. Surrounding yourself with good people can really make a difference."

For a moment, the silence between us wasn't heavy. It was still. Peaceful.

"You're stronger than you think, Ramit," she said softly. "And the right people in your life will remind you of that when you forget. And you know I'll always be there for you, no matter what."

I nodded. "Thanks, Ma."

As I stood up, I felt lighter. Not fixed. But lighter.

I looked at my phone—the date read 21 June.

Samarth's exams started today. I quickly opened our chat and recorded a voice message to wish him good luck. He had been so nervous. I hoped he did well and held on to his nerves.

I got myself ready for college. Just before leaving, I checked my phone one last time and saw two unread messages from Tamannah:

Hey Ramit. Coming to the college today?

I smiled faintly and texted back,

Yes, I am on my way.

I stepped out into the early morning warmth—the kind that lingered gently on your skin without suffocating. The kind that made you want to believe in better days. I reached college and attended all my lectures, finishing everything on my list.

The sun had begun its quiet descent by the time I found her near the arts block—journal in her hand. A breeze swept through, lifting her hair lift as if even the wind wanted to dance with her. She looked up as I approached, half-smiling, as if she already knew what I was about to say.

"Long day?" she asked, closing the journal gently.

"Yeah, pretty much," I said, sitting beside her. "You journal as well?"

"Used to," she replied. "Now I mostly write random thoughts."

Random thoughts. It made me curious. I hesitated, then asked, "Can I read some of your random thoughts? Only if you're okay with it."

She looked at me, a faint smirk on her face. She paused, then flipped a few pages and turned the journal toward me. I read slowly:

Some people dream in places.
Some in people.
I think I'm still figuring out what dreams mean to me.
But I know this much—
I want to build something that feels like sunlight for someone who's only ever known storms.

"Earlier it was journaling—pages of what happened, how I felt. Now it's more about capturing fragments. Lines that come to me when I least expect them. Some stay unfinished, some make no sense. But I like it—writing these unfinished fragments," she said, fidgeting with the pen in her hand.

"That's beautiful," I said, "It's like it bleeds... honesty."

She smiled and shrugged. "That's the thing about writing. Sometimes you don't know what you're trying to say until it's on the page."

There was a pause. A quiet one.

"So, what do you dream of building?" I asked.

She leaned her head back against the tree, eyes half closed.

"A space where people can breathe. Maybe a community home... or a small publishing house for unheard voices. Maybe a library-café where people are allowed to feel safe just being."

I watched her. Noticed the way her voice softened when she spoke about those things.

"You ever tell anyone this?" I asked.

She shook her head. "Not really. Most people expect answers like MBA, job, abroad."

"You know what? You'd be incredible at building something like that."

She looked at me. And for a moment, something shifted in the air between us. Not romance. Not confusion. Just... understanding.

"Maybe that's why we met," she said softly. "To remind each other that we're allowed to dream differently."

She took the journal notebook from my hand and jotted down the words she had just said—but in a different and modified manner.

Some people are destined to meet, to remind each other that we're allowed to dream. Dream out of the box.

25

Chapter Twenty-Five

A Week Later – 28 July, 2024

"There was someone I used to call a brother once," I said, not entirely sure why now felt like the time to bring him up. Maybe it was the way Tamannah looked at me—like she already knew there were missing pages in my story.

She didn't press for more. She just looked at me, her eyes softening, waiting patiently for me to take my time and find the courage to share the rest. I wasn't sure if I wanted to. Talking about what had happened between me and Ayush was difficult—it felt like swallowing a stone.

"You two drifted apart, didn't you?" she asked quietly, her voice threading into the spaces between my thoughts.

I nodded slowly, trying to gather my thoughts. "We did... over something stupid. At least, that's how it feels now. Back then, it was a lot more complicated than that."

"I get that," she said, almost to herself. "People leave and come back into our lives, and sometimes we have no idea why or how it happens. And the ones who leave... they take parts of us with them."

"Yeah," I said softly. "But sometimes... when they leave, it's like they take a piece of you that you can never get back. You don't realize it until you've already let them go. It's too late till by then."

There was a quiet pause, and I could feel her waiting for me to say more. I wasn't sure I wanted to. But for some reason, I felt like I had to explain. I told her everything that had happened between me and Ayush.

"That's unfortunate, that things didn't go well between you. But maybe it happened for a reason," she said. "Even though there's this old saying, which I don't agree with—and I don't even like it—

Joh Hota Hai Achhe Ke Liye Hota Hai.
Whatever happens, happens for the good."

"I mean, it doesn't make any sense to me," I said, disappointment clearly written on my face.

"Totally agreed. It doesn't. But maybe it does, in this case? I don't know if it happened for the so-called greater good or not. But there is definitely a reason behind it," she said, leaning forward, trying to cheer me up and help me see the brighter side.

"And who knows, he might come back into your life in the near future. That's a possibility, right?" she added, raising her eyebrows.

"Right. Maybe one day," I said softly.

"One day. Maybe," she echoed, leaning back and looking up at the sky.

There was another pause when Tamannah noticed Samarth sitting in a quiet corner of the block.

"Hey, that's your friend, Samarth, right?" she asked, pointing toward him.

"Yes, that's him. What's he doing there, all alone? He doesn't seem okay." I had just finished speaking these words, when Tamannah called out Samarth's name, her voice echoing even in the busy and noisy area.

Samarth noticed and looked toward us. We both waved at him and he waved back. I gestured for him to come over. He looked at me, paused for a moment and then finally picked up his bag and belongings and began walking toward us.

"I don't know, but something seems off," she said.

"Yes, I can sense it too. His CA Inter exam results are approaching. That might be his concern."

He came near us, and we both shifted to make space for him to sit. He settled in that space, his shoulders dejected and low. We both greeted him, and then I asked, "How's everything? How were your exams?"

"I'm okay. The exams... went by. I don't really know," he said, putting on a fake smile that wasn't hard to spot. Samarth wasn't okay—not by a long shot. The stress was written all over him.

"You know, Samarth, exams are just one part of the journey," I said, trying to lighten the mood. "I'm sure you did well. Don't overthink things."

Samarth let out a shallow breath, his gaze drifting toward the ground. "I don't know, Ramit. It's just... I keep thinking, what if I didn't do enough? What if I'm not enough?"

Tamannah shifted in her seat, her voice soft but steady. "You don't have to prove anything to anyone, Samarth. You've already come so far. Results are just numbers; they don't define who you are."

He looked at her, and for a moment, his eyes softened. "Thanks, Tamannah. I don't know why I'm feeling this way. I should be more confident, right? I should be looking forward to the results... but I just can't wrap my head around it."

"See, you don't need to stress yourself. Your result doesn't define you—your hard work does. The effort you put in, that's what matters at the end of the day. Yes, results are important, but even if we don't succeed in one try, it's okay. There's always a new opportunity. We just need to grab it at the right moment. Keep trying hard, and you'll get it—one day or another," I said, trying my best to lift his mood.

I could feel the tension in the air, but Tamannah's presence seemed to have a calming effect on him. She wasn't saying much, but her words had this quiet power that made him listen.

"Look," Tamannah said, trying to steer the conversation in a more positive direction, "Why don't we go grab something to eat? There's this café not far from here, and I swear, their chocolate cake is magic. It'll help you take your mind off things, if just for a little while."

Samarth gave me a hesitant look, but his lips curled slightly at the mention of food. "Chocolate cake, huh? That might work."

Tamannah chuckled, nudging him lightly. The three of us stood up, stretching out the stiffness from our legs as we made our way to the nearby café. The walk was quiet but comfortable, and for a brief moment, it felt like the world outside didn't matter—like it was just the three of us, walking together as friends, ready to escape the weight of everything. The world felt like a better place in that moment.

We sat down at a corner table by the window. As the waiter brought over our orders, we fell into a relaxed silence. Tamannah's gentle smile and quiet presence seemed to have lighten the air, and for a moment, Samarth didn't seem so lost in his own mind.

The food arrived, and as we dug in, the conversation drifted naturally.

Tamannah shifted the topic to something light-hearted. "So, what's your plan after exams, Samarth? Anything fun lined up?"

He leaned back in his chair, thinking for a moment. "Honestly? I have no idea. I've been so focused on these exams, I haven't thought past it. But I guess... I'd like to travel a bit. Maybe explore something new. How about you two?"

Tamannah raised an eyebrow, her smile playful. "I'm planning on writing a book."

I almost choked on my coffee. "Wait, seriously?"

"Yeah, why not?" she shrugged, eyes twinkling. "I've always wanted to. Maybe a collection of my thoughts or something."

Samarth and I exchanged amused glances. "A book, huh? That's impressive," I said, genuinely surprised.

Tamannah grinned. "It's a start, anyway."

The conversation shifted again. The weight that had been hanging over Samarth seemed to have lifted, and though his worries weren't completely gone, he no longer seemed consumed by them.

After a while, the café started to fill up, and the evening began to settle into the quiet hum of the city. The day was winding down, but for the first time in a long while, I felt like we were all exactly where we needed to be.

26

Chapter Twenty-Six

A Week Later – 5th August 2024

"You're not heading home already, are you?"

I turned at the sound of Tamannah's voice. She was standing under the college's old peepal tree, holding a bunch of files and her tote bag, her hair slightly ruffled by the wind.

I paused. "I was planning to. Why, are you still here?"

"Assignment submission," she said, holding up the files.

I smiled faintly, walking toward her. "You always leave it to the last moment."

She rolled her eyes playfully. "And you always leave before the best part of the day begins."

The breeze was picked up. There was something calming about that moment—college almost empty, everything slow and in between.

We started walking toward the college gate, side by side.

"So," she asked, "what's next for today? Another lonely metro ride?"

I was about to respond when I heard it—a group of students behind us, one of them saying a little too loudly—

"CA Inter ka result aa gaya kya?"

I stopped walking.

Tamannah noticed. "What happened?"

I didn't respond immediately. I just pulled out my phone, a strange, hollow pit forming in my stomach.

1 new message from Samarth.

I opened it.

"Thank you for everything. Sorry."

The words stared back at me—simple and terrifying.

My fingers froze. For a moment, all sound faded. Then Tamannah's voice broke through—

"Ramit? What happened?"

I showed her the screen.

Her face turned pale. "Where is he right now?"

"I don't know," I whispered. "His hostel, maybe."

And then—I ran.

I didn't remember what I shouted to Tamannah before I took off, or whether I even said anything at all. All I knew was that I had to reach Samarth. I sprinted past the college gate, weaving through the rush of students and auto-rickshaws, my backpack thudding against my back with every step.

My thoughts were racing. *He wouldn't... No, he couldn't...*

I tried calling him. Not once, not twice—thrice. **No response.**

My phone just rang again and again, until it went dead silent.

Goddammit, pick up! Please, pick up, pick up...

I didn't stop running. I was out of breath and my legs were trembling. I caught an auto, barely explaining anything to the driver, except for the location.

"Bhaiya, jaldi! Jaldi chalo, bas ab!"

He must've sensed something in my voice and body language because he didn't ask any questions. He just drove off quickly without further inquiry.

I tried calling Samarth again. Still nothing.

Then I messaged him, with shaking hands.

"Samarth, where are you? Please talk to me. I'm on my way. Please don't do anything stupid. Please."

No blue ticks.

I kept refreshing WhatsApp, kept trying to reach him.

We reached the hostel.

I didn't wait for the auto to stop completely. I jumped out, ran past the security guard, ignoring his calls. I didn't wait for the lift. I took the stairs two at a time. *Third floor... Room 34.*

My chest was burning.

I reached the door. Locked from the inside.

I banged on it. "Samarth! Samarth, open the door!"

Nothing.

Then—something.

A creaking sound.

No... no...

A crowd of hostel students and hostel staff gathered around me, watching the scene unfold.

"Samarth!" I rammed my shoulder into the door.

Again.

Again.

Until it burst open.

And I saw him.

He was hanging from the ceiling fan.

A chair was tipped over nearby. His room was a mess. A note lay on the bed. And Samarth—unmoving, swaying gently.

I didn't know what happened to me in that moment. Everything went blank. My body moved before my brain could register. I rushed to him, scrambled for anything—a stool, a chair, *my hands*—anything to lift him up.

A few students rushed in. One of them ran to the kitchen, grabbed a knife, and cut through the bedsheet rope with steady hands.

He collapsed into my arms like a ragdoll. I held him, checked his breath and pulse.

Faint. But it was there.

"Samarth, don't you dare die on me. Not today. Stay with me!" I yelled.

The others helped me to carry him outside. Somebody had already called an ambulance, but I knew it would take time. As we reached the ground floor, I saw the same auto-rickshaw driver waiting.

"*Aao, mai le chalta hoon. Ambulance aane mein time lagega,*" he said.

I rushed Samarth inside. One of the hostel guys asked me if he could come with me, just in case, I nodded. He sat in the front, next to the driver.

I held Samarth's hand, constantly checking for a pulse. His head rested on my lap. The auto rickshaw driver ignored traffic rules, and the guy in the front helped clear the way.

We reached the hospital.

The three of us carried Samarth out of the auto as I shouted for a stretcher. A guard ran inside to call someone. I held Samarth until the stretcher arrived.

His face had turned pale, his lips a frightening shade of blue.

A stretcher arrived. I placed him on it gently. Nurses scrambled.

"What happened?" one of them asked.

"Suicidal attempt. Hanging," I replied in a voice that didn't sound like mine.

They wheeled him away faster than I could follow. A nurse held me back as I tried to enter the ICU.

"Please, wait outside. We'll do everything we can."

I nodded, numb.

And then—I just stood there.

Body trembling. T-shirt soaked in sweat. Throat as dry as a desert.

I slowly slid down the wall and sat on the floor outside the ICU doors. The hallway buzzed with medical urgency, but inside my head—just silence.

Everything replayed again and again—his limp body, the rope, the chair, that *thank you* text.

"*Thank you for everything. Sorry.*"

That message was still there. Time-stamped 3:26 PM.

A lump rose in my throat. My chest collapsed inward. My breath caught, and the tears came—silent, at first, then sharp and gasping. I didn't care who was watching. I had almost lost him. I had almost—

My phone buzzed in my hand. It was Tamannah.

I gathered some strength to answer.

I swiped and brought the phone to my ear.

"Hello? Ramit? Is everything okay?"

I didn't say anything. I couldn't. I just cried and cried. The gasps grew louder. The tears rolled down my cheeks.

"Ramit, say something! I'm so worried. What happened?!" Her voice rose— this was the first time I'd heard her yell.

I gathered some courage. "Sam tried to take his own life. I'm currently at the Jeevan Deep Hospital, sitting outside the ICU, holding on to dear life."

"Oh my god! I'll be there in no time. Just wait." She ended the call before I could say anything else.

I stood up and sat in a chair nearby. I hadn't processed it yet. The image of Samarth's lifeless body still floated in my head—his feet barely touching the floor, the slow creak of the fan, the half-empty water bottle on his desk. I didn't know how I'd brought him down. My arms had gone numb halfway.

My hands were still cold. I couldn't remember the last time I'd felt so helpless.

Then—I heard footsteps. Fast. Urgent.

I didn't even need to look.

Tamannah.

She appeared around the corner, slightly out of breath, eyes scanning the corridor until they landed on me. Her expression changed instantly—relief, worry, confusion—all at once.

She walked straight to me. "Ramit…"

I looked up. "He's inside. Still unconscious. They're not saying anything yet."

She sat beside me, placing a gentle hand on mine. "What exactly happened?"

"I knew something was wrong. I rushed to his hostel… and found him… hanging. I don't know how I did it, but I brought him down. I screamed for help. Got him here."

A heavy silence settled between us.

"He always hid it so well," I whispered. "He laughed with us, cracked jokes… and this was happening right under our noses."

Tamannah's voice was soft. "People like him… they give everything to the world and keep nothing for themselves."

I looked at her. There was something in her gaze—like she'd lived this pain before. She understood more than she was said.

After a pause, she asked, "Did he leave anything? A note?"

I nodded. "Yes. On his bed. But I didn't get time to check it."

Tamannah's voice grew firmer. "He needs to know he's not alone. He needs to know people *see* him."

"I know," I nodded. "I'll be there for him. No matter what."

Just then, a doctor stepped out. We both stood instantly.

"He's stable," the doctor said. "It was close, but we managed to revive him. He's unconscious for now, but out of danger."

Relief surged through me. My knees almost gave in.

"Can we see him?" I asked.

"I'm sorry, not yet. We're still checking on him."

"It's okay. I'll handle the formalities," I said.

The doctor patted my back and left. I moved forward, peeking through the ICU window.

He was there, surrounded by machines. Breathing shallow but steady.

You're still here, Samarth. You're still here. I whispered as a tear slipped down my cheek.

Stable.

That's what the doctor had said.

But what about everything else?

What about the pain Samarth had carried for months?

What about every time he said he was "okay"?

I ran a hand over my face, brushing off sweat and tears I hadn't realised were there.

The hospital was quieter now. Or maybe my mind had.

People passed by. Nurses with clipboards. Relatives clutching hope like prayer beads. But all of it blurred at the edges.

I could've lost him. His parents could've lost their son.

That thought settled like a rock on my chest.

I kept asking myself—**Why didn't I see it?**

All those times he'd been quiet—was he drowning?

Didn't I do enough? Didn't we?

And the worst part?

I knew this feeling.

This hollowness.

This ache that curls up inside and eats you quietly from within.

I'd been there—last May. After Mayanti. After Ayush.

And yet, even with all that pain fresh inside me, I couldn't see his. What does that say about me?

I leaned my head back against the wall, eyes shut tight.

How many thank-yous have we missed in life that weren't really thanks, but warnings in disguise?

I swallowed the lump in my throat.

"I keep thinking..." I began, then faltered.

She waited, shoulder barely touching mine.

"I keep thinking how I didn't see it. How I couldn't tell. I should've known something was wrong."

Tamannah turned to me. "You're not a mind reader, Ramit. You're human. And so is he. We all hide things we don't want the world to see."

She placed something in my hands. A paper cup of tea.

"It's terrible, by the way," she said. "But it's hot."

I gave her a faint smile and wrapped my fingers around it.

"I don't know what comes next," I admitted. "What I'll even say to him when he wakes up. What'll I tell his parents."

"You'll say what you always do," she said softly. "You'll show up. You'll be there."

She looked at me, eyes sincere. "You already saved his life, Ramit. Now just... keep being in it."

"I was scared," I confessed, barely above a whisper. "I thought I was going to lose another person."

Tamannah placed her hand gently on mine.

"You didn't."

27

Chapter Twenty-Seven

Ayush didn't speak for a while after I finished. His gaze had shifted to somewhere beyond the restaurant window, watching nothing in particular. The silence between us wasn't uncomfortable—it was just... heavy.

Across the table, Samarth sat quietly too. This was the first time they had met, and it wasn't exactly the kind of introduction people hoped for.

"I didn't know," Ayush finally said, his voice a whisper. "I didn't know any of this, Ramit."

I gave a soft nod. "I never told you. There was too much happening. And... you weren't around."

Ayush didn't flinch, but the words settled somewhere in him. "Yeah," he murmured. "I wasn't."

He turned to Samarth and held out his hand. "I... I don't even know what to say except—I'm really glad you're still here."

Samarth looked at him for a second, then shook his hand. "Thanks," he said, a little awkwardly. "I'm still figuring it all out."

"Aren't we all?" I added, trying to ease the intensity.

Ayush leaned back, exhaling slowly. "I thought I knew you," he said to me. "But I had no idea you were carrying all this alone."

"You weren't supposed to," I replied. "It wasn't your burden anymore. After everything that happened..."

I stopped myself. The past was still tender.

Samarth looked at both of us, then spoke. "I don't know much about what happened between you two. But if it's anything like what I've seen with Ramit... he doesn't shut the world out until it shuts him out first."

That landed. Even I felt it.

Ayush looked at me again, softer now. "Let's not stay strangers," he said.

I nodded. "That's all I wanted."

There was a small pause after I said those words. Then Ayush leaned forward and said, "You know? I still remember a couple of instances. When Ramit used to tell me about you, Samarth. I didn't know much about you, or anything at all. But one thing I did know—he really cared for you and considered you a brother."

I looked at Samarth, and he held my hand firmly as he listened to Ayush continue, "I don't know if you realise it fully, but you played an important role in Ramit's life back then."

I smiled. "He's right. You were like a missing piece in the puzzle of my life... Still are. I don't know what would've happened if I lost—"

I stopped. My voice almost cracked. Samarth stood up and came closer to me. He made me stand up and embraced me tightly.

"Do you even realize your importance in my life? I almost took my life that day... But then, you came in, smashed that door, and saved me. How could I ever repay that debt?"

"You don't. That's the point. I just did what anyone else would've done in that situation."

"Not just 'anyone else'. You're more than that. A brother. Thank you, Ramit. I'm still grateful for you," he said, with teary eyes.

Ayush watched both of us, sitting there quietly, noticing the moment between us.

I wiped my eyes and said, "Let's not get sentimental now. Enough of the tears."

We didn't say much after that.

The air between us was heavy, but in a way that felt like a burden lifting.

Samarth had always been there for me in his own quiet way. Even before the suicide attempt, there had always been a bond—even if I never fully acknowledged. And now, this—this newfound understanding between the three of us—it felt like the missing piece I never knew I needed.

"You know, when I first saw you with Samarth today," Ayush said, "I couldn't help but think... we're all so different, in our own ways. But I guess that's what makes us work. At least, in this moment." He looked between me and Samarth.

"You both have your own battles, your own struggles. But somehow, you've helped each other through them. Even when you didn't realize it."

It was just the three of us, sitting at that table, in our shared understanding.

Ayush cleared his throat, breaking the moment. "I'm not sure how to end this conversation, so I guess I'll just say it like this: I'm sorry, Ramit. For everything I missed. For not being there when you needed someone. And Samarth..." He turned to him with a smile that was both warm and apologetic. "I'm glad you're here. It's not about the past, really—it's about what we make of now. This could be the start of a new friendship, right?" He offered a handshake to Samarth.

"Right. Let's build on to that. We'll do it."

I found my voice again. "Okay, enough with the heavy stuff. I think it's time for some stupid, overpriced dessert, don't you think?"

Ayush laughed, shaking his head. "Only if I'm paying."

I raised an eyebrow. "You're paying?"

"Yeah. My treat. Consider it my apology for being a clueless jerk for all these years."

I chuckled. "Well, if you insist—and don't call yourself a jerk. Please."

And just like that, the air lightened. We stood up, the tension from before fading away, replaced by the easy banter that had always been the cornerstone of our friendship.

Old bonds were being revived.

New ones were just beginning.

Maybe things weren't perfect.

Maybe we weren't whole.

But we were moving forward.

Together.

28

Chapter Twenty-Eight

Present Day — Ramit's Car, Late Evening

The city moved past us in a blur of lights. I kept my eyes on the road, both hands on the wheel, but my mind... it was still back there, in that restaurant, in that moment with Samarth and Ayush.

Ayush sat beside me in the passenger seat, unusually quiet. The night felt like a slow exhale.

"I still can't wrap my head around it," he said finally. "How close it was. How easy it is to lose someone. Just like that."

I nodded. "That's the thing. It doesn't knock. It just walks in."

He turned to me. "What do you think pushed him that far?"

I didn't answer immediately. Not because I didn't know—but because I did. Too well.

"It's never just one thing," I said after a pause. "It's years of silence. Pressure that builds, unnoticed. The failure wasn't the trigger. It was the final breaking point."

Ayush looked out of the window. "Makes you think how many people carry that weight around without anyone ever noticing."

"Yeah," I said. "Samarth was always trying to hold it together. For his parents, for himself. But the cracks were already there."

There was silence again between us, though it didn't feel heavy.

"Did you ever feel like giving up on life? Like Samarth did?" I asked him, wondering how he had coped during his tough phases.

He didn't answer immediately. He looked at the street lamps above us, lost in thought.

"I have. But I knew I would never take that step. I would rather live a miserable life than leave my parents crying over my lifeless body. I can't even imagine that," he said, taking out his wallet from his hip pocket and looking at the picture of him and his parents in it.

"Life is much more than failures. A failure doesn't define you. It can never define you."

And then I said, almost to myself, "You know, the day he opened his eyes in the hospital... that's when I realised how much of him I could've lost."

Ayush looked at me again. "What happened after that? I mean—his parents, everything?"

I didn't answer with words right away. Instead, I let the memory come.

ᕦᕦᕦ

Past – August 2024
Jeevan Deep Hospital – ICU Waiting Area

I had been pacing the corridor outside the ICU for what felt like hours, my eyes flicking now and then to the closed door behind which Samarth lay—alive, but unconscious.

Machines beeped. Nurses moved like clockwork. Tamannah had stepped out to get some coffee, leaving me alone with the weight of everything that had just happened.

Then, the elevator chimed.

I turned, and there they were—Samarth's parents. His mother looked as if she hadn't blinked since hearing the news, and his father... stoic, but broken behind the eyes.

"Ramit?" his father said, almost unsure of how to begin.

I stepped forward. "Yes, Uncle."

He didn't say anything for a few seconds. Then he simply walked up to me and placed a trembling hand on my shoulder.

"Thank you... I don't know how to—thank you for saving my son."

Samarth's mother took a step closer. "They said you found him. You brought him here in time."

I nodded, unable to say much. "He's still under observation... but the doctors said the worst is over."

Her eyes welled up. "He's always kept things to himself. We never thought... we didn't know it was that bad."

I looked down. "He didn't want to disappoint you."

She covered her mouth with one hand as the tears fell freely now. His father stepped in and held her close. "We'll get him through this," he whispered to her. "Together."

Then he turned back to me, steadier now. "You were there when we couldn't be. That means more than anything. You're family now, Ramit. You always were."

Tamannah returned with two cups in her hand, her eyes widening slightly at the sight of Samarth's parents. She approached quietly, reading the moment with perfect intuition.

"Uncle, Aunty... I'm Tamannah. I was with Ramit when... when everything happened," she said softly.

They acknowledged her with quiet gratitude.

After a while, a nurse came out with an update. Samarth was stable. Still sedated, but stable.

Samarth's mother closed her eyes and whispered a silent prayer.

"You should go and meet him now. He'll feel better. We'll take your leave now. Take care of yourselves— and of Sam," I said to Samarth's parents.

"Thank you, beta. We can't express our gratitude towards you at the moment. Stay in touch. Take care," Samarth's mother said, cupping my face gently in her hands.

I gave her a faint smile. They left us, entering the ICU unit where Samarth was being cared for.

We stepped out of the hospital building just as the sky began to change. That soft violet stretch of twilight had taken over, and the air carried a quiet chill. Tamannah walked beside me, not saying much at first. It had been an emotionally charged day.

The faint sounds of Delhi traffic hummed in the distance. A dog barked somewhere. Life, outside these walls, had continued as usual. But not for us.

"You okay?" Tamannah finally asked, her voice gentle.

I nodded. "Yeah. I think so. Just... trying to let it all sink in."

She didn't press further. Instead, she matched her steps with mine—slow and steady.

"His parents..." I started, my voice trailing off.

"They were kind," she said. "And broken. In that way only parents can be when they realise how close they came to losing a child."

I exhaled, rubbing the back of my neck. "I never thought I'd be in a situation like this. Holding someone's life together, even for a second. It makes you think."

"Think what?"

"How fragile everything really is," I said. "One missed call. One ignored message. One evening where no one notices you've gone quiet—and suddenly, things fall apart."

She was quiet again for a moment. Then she said, "I've always believed people don't just break. They crack slowly, over time. We just don't notice until something shatters."

We reached the edge of the hospital parking lot. I stopped, turning to her slightly.

"I'm glad you were there today," I said. "I don't think I could've handled it alone."

"I didn't do much."

"You showed up. That's more than most people do."

She smiled, her eyes soft now. "You're not alone, Ramit. Even if it feels like that sometimes."

I nodded, swallowing down a strange lump forming in my throat.

We walked back toward the gate, and as we did, I found myself thinking of something Professor Anand had once said:

You never know when the invisible string between two people will pull them back together—or snap completely.

For now, all I could do was keep walking forward, one step at a time.

ϸϸϸ

The road ahead was quiet, broken only by the occasional flicker of streetlights and the steady rhythm of the car's tires humming over asphalt. Ayush sat beside me, thoughtful, his gaze wandering out the window. Neither of us spoke much after that conversation.

And I thought of the walk back from the hospital with Tamannah—the way her presence had steadied me, grounded me in ways I hadn't even understood back then.

I stared ahead, at the blinking signal, and thought:

Life never gives warnings. Just moments.

Moments that become memory, that become stories, that become scars.

And sometimes... strings.

Unseen, but always there.

When the light turned green, I drove forward.

Quietly.

Gratefully.

With the lingering feeling that not everything broken stays that way forever.

29

Chapter Twenty-Nine

May 2025

It's strange, this feeling of being close to something new. Graduation is just around the corner, but it doesn't feel like I've reached an endpoint. More like a continuation.

Somehow, after everything that's happened, I can't help but think life might still be leading me somewhere I can't quite picture yet. I've learned so much—more than I ever imagined I would. Who would have thought a year ago, I'd be sitting here today, with a novel nearly finished and a future ahead that feels less uncertain than before?

My bonds with people like Samarth and Tamannah are stronger than ever. Almost a year ago, I thought I had lost enough people in my life, when Samarth attempted to take his own life. That day, I realized the role of the people we care about—the people who care about us. These bonds are what we are truly made of, and this is what makes us who we actually are.

To think about it—the invisible string theory. No one can tell when two strings are going to pull each other back or snap away completely, forever. That's the unpredictability of life.

You never know what might happen the next day. I've learned to live in the moment. Maybe not completely, but I have—to some extent.

I've been more grateful for the people who make my life better every single day. I am grateful for this life God has given to me. I don't blame or curse anyone for the lows in life anymore. I feel thankful for each moment that's worth living for.

I went through a very tough phase last year, which lasted for three to four months. After that, I backed myself and conquered my battles fiercely. I excelled in my studies and improved my grades in college. I've almost published a novel—on my own, quietly. I can now see the path I'm destined to walk on. Not clearly, but the future doesn't seem as uncertain anymore.

After such a long time, I am happy. I truly am. I'm going to publish my novel very soon. Mumma would be so proud of me. I can't wait for the day now—a dream I had when I was seven years old is now on the verge of being fulfilled.

I'm not ready for my college life to end. I was thinking about it the other day when I saw the final examination date sheet.

In a couple of weeks, all of this will be over. No more study sessions with friends. No more auto-rickshaw rides from the metro station to college. No more meeting classmates on a regular basis. Nothing. It'll all be gone.

Everyone will get busy with their lives and start walking their respective paths. I'm not ready for that. It'll feel like a new start—a reset. My eyes well up, thinking about the days and memories I've created within the red walls of my college building. All of this will be gone.

I truly hope my roads will keep diverging again and again with the roads of the people I care for and want to create core memories with. I don't want to lose them—especially Sam and Tamannah. They held me through thick and thin, and it's my duty to do the same for the rest of our lives. They are very close to my heart.

A lot of people will move out of my life. It makes me sad. But that's the beauty of it. The way I've started to look at it—or at least, try to—is that we will go on and get busy with our pursuits. But wherever we go, we will take a piece of each other with us. We will carry that piece into everything that we do next—to remind us of who we are, and of who we're meant to be.

I miss the people I couldn't hold on to over the last two or three years. I wonder what they're up to these days. Has life been kind to them?

I miss Mayanti. I still do. I can never forget her. I hope she's healthy and doing well, wherever she is. I love her so much—and always will.

Ayush—a friend I made on the first day of college. Things didn't end well between us, and no attempts were made to sort things out.

Their memories still make me cry up occasionally, to this date. I try to move on, but I can't. Or maybe I just don't want to. Is that something I should be proud of? Maybe not. Nevertheless, I don't like moving on. I never liked the idea of it.

I still don't know, if both of them were a passing chapter in my life or something more than that.

Maybe, one day, I'll see them again. I'll talk to them again. That's the beauty of life—it's unpredictable in so many ways. I hope to see them again. I truly do. I'm someone who believes in keeping hope, even at the worst stages of life.

"Sometimes, the invisible strings between us stretch across time and silence—pulling us closer when we least expect it, or snapping away without warning, leaving echoes where a bond once lived."

30

Chapter Thirty

4th June, 2025 – Tamannah's Residence

I had always liked the way evenings fell in Delhi. The chaos softened a little, the light turned golden, and for a brief moment, the world felt... quieter. Not silent, just *still* — like the city had paused to think.

Outside, the air smelled like summer dust and blooming gulmohars. My bag was packed, phone charged. Everything was in place. Still, I checked twice.

I tied my hair in a loose knot, staring into the mirror. There was something in my eyes that I couldn't name. It wasn't sadness. It wasn't joy either.

Life moved like it always did—urgent, unaware.

I grabbed my belongings and paused at the door.

Just a second.

I wasn't sure why, but something in me wanted to stay still for a breath longer. Maybe it was just nerves. Maybe it was instinct. Or maybe it was nothing at all.

I looked around the room. Books on the shelf, coffee mug on the desk, the soft rustle of curtains brushing the window sill. Everything felt *in place*, and somehow... far away.

"Stop being dramatic," I muttered under my breath, trying to smile.

I went downstairs and booked a cab.

The streets felt different. A street vendor struggled to arrange his items in an organized way. A group of school kids ran past, their laughter trailing behind. Life moved fast. It never failed to fascinate me.

My cab arrived just two minutes early. The driver glanced up as I approached, offering a small nod. I nodded back, pulling the strap of my bag tighter over my shoulder.

I took one last glance at the sky. The sun was dipping low, a ribbon of orange stretched across the horizon.

Funny how familiar everything looked. And yet, something about that evening felt different.

I opened the door and stepped inside.

A soft click as it shut.

The engine purred to life.

And just like that, the world began to blur.

The road ahead stretched wide, unknowable.

31

Chapter Thirty-One

7th June, 2025

Something was off.

It wasn't the weather—though the morning felt unusually still, as if even the Delhi summer had hit pause. It wasn't the usual metro ride either—though the voices around me on the train felt more distant than usual. It was something I couldn't name. A silence inside me that hadn't been there before.

Tamannah hadn't replied to my last message. I had texted her two days ago, just to check in.

"How did your work go? Want to catch up this weekend?"

She had mentioned something about going out for an important work on the 4th. But she never said how long she'd be gone. And she had never left without replying for this long.

Still, I kept brushing off the unease. Maybe she was just caught up. Maybe it was one of those intensive volunteering days she used to talk about. Or maybe I was overthinking again, like I used to.

At college, I scanned the corridor out of habit. The department walls were plastered with notices. But my eyes weren't searching for announcements. They were scanning for a familiar silhouette—Tamannah, with her worn-out tote bag, waving at me from down the hall like she always did.

She wasn't there.

10:30 AM.

First lecture done.

Still no sign of her.

By noon, something inside me had started to tighten.

During lunch, I sat under the neem tree where she once sat with me for hours, talking about her transfer from Miranda House, her dreams, her habit of writing random thoughts in her journal for comfort. The spot was empty today.

I scrolled through our chat, but the last message I had sent still hadn't turned blue.

I messaged Samarth.

"Have you heard from Tamannah? She hasn't been to college for a few days."

He replied almost immediately.

"I thought she was with you? She said she had some work outside Delhi. But it's weird. I haven't heard anything either."

That was the first moment I felt it—panic, quiet and creeping, like a shadow rising behind me.

I walked across the building. I passed the English Honours room. A few students were gathered near the notice board. I wasn't going to stop. I didn't even know why I slowed down.

But I heard it.

A name.

Her name.

"She passed away... in a car accident. It was on the 4th," one of the girls said softly.

I froze.

No. No, I must have misheard that. Maybe it was someone else. Tamannah wasn't a rare name. Maybe it was another student. Maybe—

"Tamannah Sharma," the other girl murmured, her voice lowered in disbelief. "It was the same day she left for that NGO assignment. The news was on the department group... Didn't you see?"

My world tilted.

I don't remember how I got closer to them. I don't remember asking the question, but I heard my voice before I felt it.

"Tamannah… died?"

They turned to me slowly, recognizing me.

"I'm sorry," one of them said, eyes wide with sudden guilt.

"We thought you knew. She met with an accident near the outskirts… The car flipped, they said. She didn't make it to the hospital."

I didn't say a word.

I just walked.

I walked past the canteen, past the courtyard, past the last bench where she and I had once shared lunch when we both forgot to bring tiffin.

I walked into an empty classroom and sat down at the farthest desk.

And then it hit me.

The silence. The unread messages. The absence that hadn't made sense.

She was gone.

Tears didn't come immediately. Instead, I went numb. I stared at the chair across from me. My mind kept trying to picture her in that moment—getting into the car, adjusting her bag, playing some Hindi song on loop.

Was she scared? Was she alone?

I pulled out my phone again, staring at our messages.

"Let's go to that new bookstore next week?"

This was it, then. This was the moment people write about. When your life splits into before and after. When the string snaps—not with noise, but with silence.

The walls blurred at the edges of my vision, and for a moment, I forgot how to breathe.

My hands were trembling when I reached for my phone again. I didn't think. I didn't plan. I just hit the call button beside *Samarth's* name.

He picked up after the first ring.

"Hello?"

I couldn't speak.

"Ramit? You there?"

I pressed the phone closer to my ear, but no words came. Just air. Stuck in my lungs like glass.

"Ramit, are you okay? What happened?"

And then it cracked.

"Sam..."

My voice broke, shattering into something unrecognizable. "She's gone."

There was silence on the other end.

I was already crying by then. No—sobbing. The kind of crying you can't hold in, that doesn't wait for permission. My shoulders heaved, and I could barely sit upright. The grief crashed like a wave I hadn't seen coming, swallowing me whole.

"She's... Tamannah... she died in an accident. On the 4th. I just found out. No one told me, Sam. No one told me anything."

I didn't realize I was screaming until I heard myself.

"I *messaged* her! I asked her how her work went—I was waiting for her reply! I thought she was busy! I thought—God, I thought she'd be back, she always comes back—"

"Ramit..." Samarth's voice cracked too. "No... no, that can't be true."

"It is!" I wept into the phone. "She's gone, Sam. She's really gone."

And in that moment, he didn't say anything else.

He just cried with me.

No consolations. No words. Just two friends, broken, on either end of a phone call—grieving someone they loved in different ways, and lost in the same way.

Time collapsed around us.

I wasn't in that classroom anymore.

I wasn't anywhere.

ϷϷϷ

13th August, 2024

Samarth lay propped up on the bed, pale but alive. The drip clicked quietly beside him. Ramit sat near his feet, and Tamannah had pulled up a stool next to the bed, her chin resting on her palm.

It was late. The kind of late where even the machines seemed to hum softer.

"No one tells you how weird it feels to still be here," Samarth said suddenly, voice raspy but clearer than it had been in days.

Tamannah didn't react immediately. She let the silence stretch, giving the words space to breathe.

"We're glad you're still here," she said softly.

Samarth smiled, but it didn't reach his eyes.

"Yeah. But for a while there... I didn't want to be. That version of me is hard to shake off."

Ramit shifted, his throat tightening. "You don't have to go back there, Sam. We're past that."

Tamannah leaned forward, looking at both of them. "You know what I've been thinking?" she said.

"Death isn't the scariest thing. It's disappearing quietly. Like... having lived this entire life, and then just fading. No echoes, no legacy. Just silence."

Ramit met her gaze, something unsettled blooming in his chest.

"You think about that a lot?"

She shrugged, a little smile on her lips. "Sometimes. It's why I want to leave something behind. Even if it's small. A gesture, a story, a memory. Something."

Samarth's eyes fluttered shut, and he murmured,

"You already have."

Ramit had wanted to believe that too. That the things they did—these small, quiet acts—mattered more than they thought in the grand scheme.

"I hope," Tamannah said after a moment, "if I ever disappear one day... someone will remember the good parts. Not the way I go. Just the way I made them feel."

And then she smiled.

The memory shattered like glass in Ramit's mind.

Now, in the silence of the college corridor, his knees gave way as the weight of that moment came rushing back with unbearable clarity.

She had said it, word for word.
And now... she had disappeared.
Gone forever.
Faded.

32

Chapter Thirty-Two

July 2025 – Ramit's Home, Evening

The world had a way of continuing, even when it should have stopped. The fan above me spun in lazy circles, casting slow, slanted shadows across the ceiling. Outside, children laughed in the distance—carefree, as they should be. But inside, everything had gone still. Except the ache.

I hadn't stepped out of my room in hours. Maybe days. Time had blurred. My phone lay dead on the bedside table, untouched. Samarth had texted, called—I couldn't bring myself to read anything. I wasn't ready to talk. How do you talk when your heart refuses to believe what it already knows?

The door creaked open, and I didn't have to look to know it was Mumma.

She stood quietly at the threshold, hesitant. "Khaana rakha hai, beta," she said softly, placing the plate on my study table.

I gave a faint nod, eyes fixed on the notebook in my lap. She lingered for a moment longer, as if wanting to say something. But instead, she simply walked over and placed a gentle hand on my head.

"I know she meant a lot," she whispered, brushing my hair back. "Take your time."

And then she left.

The door clicked shut behind her, and I was alone again. Me, my grief, and a sea of memories I wasn't ready to wade through.

I picked up my pen and opened my journal.

"The world didn't stop, Tamannah. How unfair is that? I'm still here, breathing, writing, aching... and you're not. How does absence echo louder than presence?"

I paused, the ink blotting at the edge of the sentence.

"You said once that disappearing without a sound is worse than death. But you didn't disappear, did you? Not from me. You've etched yourself into every corner of my life. Every chai break. Every sarcastic comment. Every smile I didn't realize I depended on until it stopped arriving."

My hands trembled. I gripped the pen tighter.

"I wasn't ready. None of us were. You were supposed to stay longer. We were supposed to celebrate graduation, argue over book titles, figure life out together."

I reached for the envelope she had once left in my notebook—a doodle of the three of us. She'd sketched it after one of our late-night hostel sessions. Stick figures, terrible shading, and hearts above our heads.

"If you ever disappear, Tamannah... I swear, I'll never let the world forget how you made it feel."

A tear fell onto the paper, smudging the ink slightly. I let it.

Tonight, I would write until it hurt less.

And even if it never did, I'd keep writing.

Because some people don't leave behind gravestones.

They leave behind stories.

And Tamannah...

She was one hell of a story.

Mumma's words still lingered, soft in my mind: *"Take your time."*

She wasn't the one who had to fill the empty space beside me.

She didn't have to hold onto the silence that now stretched endlessly between my thoughts.

I was used to silence. But this one... this one was deafening.

My pen scratched across the page again. I couldn't stop writing. It wasn't even about forming coherent sentences anymore. It was about moving my hand, making words come out. Something to keep me grounded in the midst of this overwhelming weight.

It wasn't that I hadn't cried enough already. It was just that, with every passing moment, the absence of her grew more unbearable.

I kept writing. My thoughts spilled onto the page with no particular order. They didn't need order. All I had to do was let them out.

I paused, wiping my eyes again, only for more tears to slip down my face. The words didn't feel enough. They never would. I could write for days, weeks, years, but the hole inside me would remain.

A car accident. Just like that. Life taken in the blink of an eye.

How could something so fragile, so unpredictable, change the course of everything?

My phone buzzed on the table beside me. Samarth's name flashed across the screen.

I let it ring.

I wasn't ready to talk to anyone. I didn't have words for them. Not today. Maybe not ever.

Another tear fell, and I scribbled over it with my pen, the ink running in messy streaks.

"Do you even know what you've left behind? How much of you was stitched into the very fabric of my life? How do I continue without you? I thought I was strong. I thought I had the answers. But I don't. Not anymore. Not without you here."

I closed the journal for a moment, resting my forehead against it, feeling the weight of the paper on my skin—the weight of everything.

33

Chapter Thirty-Three

Present Day – January 2032

The sky stretched out in front of me as the sun slowly made its descent behind the horizon. The air was quiet, and the emptiness of the field around us felt comforting, like the whole world was holding its breath. The three of us stood at the edge of the open space, cars parked a little further back, their engines cooling. We didn't speak at first. There was no need to. The silence was enough.

I stared out at the horizon, trying to find a moment of peace, but all I could think about was Tamannah. Her absence had a weight I hadn't been able to shake. I felt it every day, but today, it hit harder. The empty space around us felt too much like the hole inside of me.

I felt Samarth shift beside me, his voice breaking the silence, though it came out quieter than usual. He was focused on the horizon, the same way I was.

"Tamannah. I can't stop thinking about her."

My throat tightened. "I know," I said, my voice hoarse. "I keep thinking about what she'd say if she were here. She was always so sure of everything... so sure of me."

"She made everything feel possible, didn't she? Even when things were falling apart, she believed in us. In you. In me."

She had made everything feel like it could be fixed, even when it couldn't.

"I just... I wish she could see this. The restaurant. The novels I wrote. She believed in me more than I ever believed in myself."

The sadness hung between us, but there was something else in the air now. A shift, like something was about to change.

Ayush stood there, a little apart from us, but I could feel him watching. I couldn't quite place it, but there was something different about him today.

After a moment of silence, he finally spoke, breaking through the heaviness.

"I've been thinking about this for a while," Ayush said, his voice steady but serious. He met my gaze, and there was a sincerity in his eyes that made me pay attention. "About your dream. The restaurant."

I turned toward him, confused. "What do you mean?"

He stepped closer, his hands tucked into his pockets.

"You've been doing this on your own for so long, Ramit. But you don't have to. You've carried this weight alone for too long."

I felt my chest tighten, but I didn't say anything, waiting for him to continue.

"I want to help," Ayush said, his voice softer now. "I want to invest in your restaurant. No strings attached. Not as an investor trying to get a return, but as a friend. Someone who believes in you. In this dream."

I stared at him, unable to process what he was saying. I had so many questions, but all I could do was stand there, stunned.

"Ayush, I can't let you—"

"I'm not asking for equity," he cut in, his voice firm. "I don't want a return. I just want to help you make this happen. I've seen how hard you've worked, and how much this means to you. And I think it's time you stop carrying it all alone."

I shook my head, my heart racing. "But I can do it, Ayush. I don't need—"

"Let me be a part of it, Ramit. Please. You don't have to do this by yourself," Ayush said.

I wanted to argue, to tell him I couldn't accept it, that I didn't need anyone else's help. But the truth was, a part of me didn't want to be alone anymore. Not after everything we'd been through. Not after losing Tamannah.

I looked at Samarth, who was silent now, watching me with understanding in his eyes. I could feel his support, even without him saying a word. This wasn't just about the restaurant anymore. It was about something more. Something I hadn't fully realized until now.

I let out a shaky breath. "I don't know how to thank you, Ayush. This... this means more than you know."

Ayush smiled, the kind of smile that wasn't just for show, but one that carried the weight of years of friendship.

"You don't have to thank me. Just let me be a part of this. For Sam. For Tamannah. And for you."

I could feel the tears welling up, but I held them back. This wasn't about crying anymore. It was about moving forward.

Tamannah wouldn't have wanted us to be stuck in grief forever. She'd have wanted us to keep going. She'd have wanted us to do something with the love and faith she had always shown us.

"I won't let you down," I whispered, my voice thick with emotion. "I promise."

Ayush grinned, clapping me on the back.

"I know you won't. And I'll be here with you, every step of the way."

The sun had almost disappeared behind the horizon now, leaving the sky in a deep shade of purple. The air was cooler, and the world around us felt still, like everything was waiting.

The three of us stood together in the fading light, our bond unspoken but stronger than ever. We had lost Tamannah, but we still had each other. And for the first time in a long while, I felt like I wasn't alone anymore.

As the last traces of daylight faded, I knew that things were about to change.

This was the beginning of something new.

34

Chapter Thirty-Four

July 2032 | Delhi | Book Launch Event

The lights dimmed slowly as the last question was asked. A few hands still hung in the air, but the moderator glanced at me with a smile that said, *that's a wrap.*

I nodded politely and took one last look at the crowd. Some familiar faces, some strangers. Some readers who had found pieces of themselves in my story, and some who had come along just out of curiosity.

The applause came and went, and I felt my breath steady again.

It was over.

The book was out in the world now—*all* of it.

I stepped away from the stage, walked past the last table of books stacked neatly, and exited through the side door into the late Delhi evening.

The sky was the colour of cooled embers. The breeze was just enough to remind me of change. I pulled out my car keys, ready to go home, when—

A tap.

Gentle. Just on my shoulder.

I turned.

And time blurred.

"Ramit," she said.

Just that. My name. Like she had still been holding it, all these years.

It was Mayanti.

She looked like a story paused mid-sentence. Sharp yet soft. Her hair was shorter, her presence calmer. But her eyes? The same old chaos I remembered.

"I wasn't sure if I should come," she said, smiling nervously.

I blinked once, maybe twice, to make sure this was actually happening.

"You look—"

"Different?" she offered.

"No," I said, shaking my head. "Like home, actually."

She laughed, and I could tell she hadn't expected that.

"I've been back for a month," she said. "Work brought me home. I read your book. Twice."

A pause. And then:

"I was proud. And... a little heartbroken too."

I didn't speak. Just watched her.

"I'm not here to fix anything," she added, her voice softer now.

"Just... felt like something unfinished deserved an acknowledgment. Maybe even a new beginning. If you're okay with that."

I nodded slowly, almost reflexively.

"Still unmarried?" she asked, with a lopsided smile that tried to mask how loaded the question was.

"Yeah," I said, meeting her gaze. "Still writing instead of settling."

She chuckled. "Same here. Still calculating risks for a living—just not the romantic kind."

We both laughed—briefly, quietly—before letting the silence return.

Sometimes, the universe doesn't scream. It just taps you on the shoulder.

Maybe it had been the invisible thread all along—pulling quietly, gently, through years and across continents. A thread I hadn't seen

before, but one that had always been there, waiting to be noticed.
And now that I saw it... I wasn't ready to let go.

Because sometimes, holding on to hope till the end is what makes all the difference.
And in that moment, I didn't know what came next.
But I did know this—
Some endings are actually entrances.
And maybe, just maybe, this wasn't the last page after all.

Note From The Author

(This section contains spoilers. Please read only after finishing the novel.)

First of all, I'm assuming you've finished reading the novel — because this section does contain spoilers. Here's a heartfelt letter from my side to all of you.

My Background

I've always wanted to write a book. I used to wonder how it would feel to see my name imprinted on a book cover. I'm pretty sure it feels great — and if you're reading this right now, I did it.

I grew up in an environment surrounded by literature, poetry, and books. Reading and writing have always been my coping mechanisms. My mother, an English teacher some years ago, introduced me to this world of books — and it soon became one of my biggest passions.

At the age of seven, I had a dream — to write a book or a novel, with my name on it.

Fast forward to 2025: here I am, self-publishing my debut novel. The seven-year-old me would never believe it.

ϸϸϸ

How I Started Working on It

I began working on this novel during the first semester of my college, around November 2023. It wasn't a great start, but I was determined. By February 2024, I had a properly structured story outline and began writing the first draft.

The outline wasn't perfect — nothing ever is — and I made several major changes along the way. It was a slow beginning; I'd never written a book before. But slowly and steadily, I started getting the hang of it. I learned a lot during the entire writing process.

In mid-2024, things took a downturn — my grandmother fell ill. It was a tough phase for me and my family, probably one of the worst. I couldn't devote much time to writing for the next 6–7 months, and the novel came to a halt.

By January 2025, I began picking it up again. The momentum was gone, but I still tried. Then came February, and with it, a wave of melancholy. I felt too demotivated to finish the story. I even considered changing the plot or scrapping the novel entirely.

Eventually, I took a short break, gathered myself, and decided to stay true to the original story. I resumed writing in April 2025 and pushed through the final stretch. I completed the first draft on 23rd April 2025, and then spent the next seven days editing and proofreading it.

It wasn't easy — but I wasn't going to give up either. I rushed through the editing process and submitted the final draft on 1st May 2025. I'm still trying to process how I managed to finish it all in such a short span.

My Thoughts on the Story

I think I did a decent job in coming up with a plot like this. I'm satisfied, to be honest — though it could've been better in terms of pacing and storytelling, especially towards the climax.

All the characters — Ramit, Mayanti, Samarth, Tamannah, Ayush, Anubhuti, Anand — I could relate to every single one of them. But the one that felt like a reflection of myself was Ramit. We share a lot of similarities.

Growing up, I had a rough childhood. My father was never really a father to me. I still believe the first eight years of my life left scars that shaped who I am today. Going through that kind of trauma makes you resilient. Anubhuti's character is a gift to Mumma — thank you for being my Anubhuti during those dark days.

I also had plans to explore the backstory of Professor Anand Krishnan, but I dropped the idea for some reason. I still left a subtle hint about it in the story — maybe only the keenest readers will notice.

Every character I wrote carries a piece of me, or was inspired by someone I've met in real life.

ᗏᗏᗏ

My Personal Experience

I loved writing this novel. It gave me so much joy. But I'll say this — writing a book is tough, and editing/proofreading it is a Herculean task. It was monotonous, draining, and frustrating at times.

I rushed through the final edits, so there may still be some errors in the book. I tried my best to clean it up, and if I ever spot anything, I'll fix it in future editions.

Interestingly, I never told anyone in my family that I was writing and publishing a novel. I wanted to move slowly, quietly, and surprise them when the author copies arrive. A surprise they'll remember for a long time.

Though I kept it mostly to myself, I had to share it with a few people. Thank you to those souls who knew about it. Even if I barely talked about the novel, whenever I did, you gave me a push. Each of you acted as a driving force. I mean it — thank you.

I'd also like to thank Notion Press Publishing for supporting budding authors like me. Thank you for giving me a platform to share my story with the world.

One of my biggest reasons for writing this book was simple: I felt this story needed to be told.

❦❦❦

A Final Word

I want you all to hold on to hope. Hope is a beautiful thing. Even if you lose the battle, there's always a chance to win the war. I truly believe that all is not lost until it's over. There's always a glimmer of hope — you just need to hold on.

Be it academics, career, jobs, love, friendships, or family — there's always a second chance. Don't lose it. Ever.

That's what I believe in. That's what I wanted to express through this story.

❦❦❦

Let's Stay Connected

I'd love to hear your thoughts and feedback. You can reach out to me on any social media platform. Drop a message anytime — I'd love to talk about the story, your experience, or just listen.

YouTube – @SudhitYadav
Twitter/X – @SudhitYadav
LinkedIn – Sudhit Yadav
Instagram – @Sudhit74

ᗽᗽᗽ

At Last...

I hope something in this story stays with you.
I hope you return to it again, someday.
And I hope, when you do — it feels like home.

Thank you. I mean it.

— *Sudhit Yadav*

Sudhit Yadav is a student, storyteller, and content creator based in Delhi. He completed his schooling at Bharti Public School, Mayur Vihar-III (2010-2023), and is currently pursuing a Bachelor of Commerce degree at Delhi College of Arts and Commerce, University of Delhi (2023–2026). Alongside academics, Sudhit is a YouTuber and digital creator. He has a wide range of interests across various creative and academic fields.

"Life, Destiny and the Invisible Thread" is his debut novel — a heartfelt exploration of friendship, memory, and the ties that quietly shape us.

ABOUT THE AUTHOR

www.ingramcontent.com/pod-product-compliance
Lightning Source LLC
Chambersburg PA
CBHW031041160726
47991CB00005B/1989